Lucy pulled at the wi[...]
difficulty, opened on[...]
hill was a villa. Lucy [...]
staring at it, some minutes later, when she heard a
noise. Looking down she saw, below her, a thin
man in a wheelchair. . . He looked old, but Lucy
could see that he wasn't old at all, probably in his
fifties, just terribly ill.

Feeling a bit like a voyeur, she withdrew from
the window, went over to her duffle, fished
through it and took out a small knapsack. Inside it
was her journal. She flipped through the pages. It
was full of scrapbook bits and pieces, and pictures
of her mother, including one in a long white dress
and another torn from a fashion magazine, showing Sarah modelling the sort of conventionally cut
county tweeds she would never have chosen to
wear.

Eventually Lucy found what she was looking for.
From a taped envelope she carefully extracted a
faded Polaroid of herself and Niccolo Donati sitting
close together next to a stone pillar, with steps
leading down to a lake. Lucy sat down on the bed,
looked at the snapshot for several minutes and
then slipped it under her shirt, over her heart.

Shirley Lowe has been a magazine editor and national newspaper columnist. This is her seventh book. She is the co-author, with Angela Ince, of four novels, including the best-selling *Swapping*. She is married and lives in London

STEALING BEAUTY

Shirley Lowe

ORION

An Orion paperback
First published in 1996 by
Orion Books Limited
Orion House, 5 Upper St Martin's Lane
London WC2H 9EA

A CIP catalogue record for this book is available
from the British Library

ISBN: 0 75280 687 4

Typeset by Deltatype Ltd, Birkenhead, Merseyside
Printed and bound in Great Britain by
Clays Ltd, St Ives plc

FOX SEARCHLIGHT PICTURES
RECORDED PICTURE COMPANY AND UGC IMAGES PRESENT
A JEREMY THOMAS PRODUCTION
A BERNARDO BERTOLUCCI FILM
STEALING BEAUTY

SINEAD CUSACK JEREMY IRONS JEAN MARAIS DONAL McCANN D.W. MOFFETT STEFANIA SANDRELLI AND LIV TYLER
EXECUTIVE PRODUCER FOR UGC IMAGES YVES ATTAL PRODUCTION DESIGN GIANNI SILVESTRI EDITOR PIETRO SCALIA
DIRECTOR OF PHOTOGRAPHY DARIUS KHONDJI ORIGINAL MUSIC COMPOSED AND CONDUCTED BY RICHARD HARTLEY
SCREENPLAY BY SUSAN MINOT FROM A STORY BY BERNARDO BERTOLUCCI
PRODUCED BY JEREMY THOMAS DIRECTED BY BERNARDO BERTOLUCCI

© 1996 R.P.C./UGC IMAGES/FICTION S.R.L.

CHAPTER ONE

Lucy could feel someone watching her. It was disturbingly intrusive, like the hot breath of a stranger on her cheek. She looked around the aeroplane at the other passengers but they were mostly dozing through the In Flight Entertainment and none of them seemed interested in her. She told herself to stop imagining things and gazed purposefully out of the window. The clouds parted to reveal Pisa's Piazza del Duomo and the Tower still leaning in a satisfactorily timeless sort of way.

Last time she'd been in Italy, she and her mother had climbed it together; scrabbling to the top of the tilting, uneven steps, clutching each other and giggling. Her mother had seemed so happy, then. Lucy shook her head to cancel out the memory and concentrated on gathering up her belongings and the bottle of duty free whisky she'd bought for the Graysons.

There was the usual hassle queueing to get off the plane and then she had to queue again to get through Passport Control, but finding her luggage was really easy. The old army duffle bag, tied together with string, was instantly identifiable as it trundled around the luggage terminal, nestling up against sleek Italian leatherware and brass embellished pigskin suitcases.

She grabbed the duffle and, as she turned towards the Green exit, was alarmed to see a large inquisitive dog heading her way, towing behind it a swarthy man in a businesslike uniform. Lucy stood very still. There were only a few grammes of grass in her bag. For her own personal use. She could hear herself saying those very words to the customs man. 'It's just for my own personal use, Officer.' The dog, tongue lolling expectantly, came level with her duffle and then walked straight past her and hoovered up a half-finished sandwich that was lying on the floor by her feet. Breathing out a sigh of relief, she wondered why she continued to feel uneasy. The airport was oppressively hot. She shivered. She still had the eerie feeling that she was being watched.

The man with the camera followed Lucy to the station. She bought a second class ticket to Siena. So did the man with the camera.

New York to Siena. It was a journey Lucy had taken countless times in her imagination over these past few years and it always had the same happy ending. Niccolo would take her in his arms, and although, sometimes, she couldn't quite remember the *exact* sound of his voice, he would tell her in his quirky, appealing, broken English how much he loved her and how he had longed to see her again. He would explain why he'd stopped writing (Lucy had dreamed up lots of good reasons for that. Her letters and cards had been lost in the post . . . he'd been desperately ill ... he'd gone away ...) and he'd carry her off to his villa on the hill and change her life for ever. She settled into a corner seat, adjusted her Walkman, put her feet up on her duffle and closed her eyes. She could picture him now, standing by the lake, tall and slim, with tousled dark hair and penetrating brown eyes. She could feel the way he'd kissed her, gently, persistently touching her lips with his tongue, exploring her mouth. The memory had obsessed her ever since. And now she was going to see him again.

New York to Siena. It had been a long journey and Lucy, hugging herself with anticipated pleasure, drifted into sleep. The man at the other side of the carriage lifted his video camera and studied her through his viewfinder. He saw a golden, glowing, dishevelled nineteen-year-old. Her glossy, black hair was a tumbling mess, her clothes expensively, grungily droopy and mis-matched. And wasn't there something appealingly vulnerable about the trickle of saliva at the corner of her mouth, the nakedness of the foot where one of her boots had fallen, crinkled and unpolished, onto the carriage floor, the hands hanging loosely, innocently, in her crotch? The man smiled unpleasantly as he lowered his camera. The train was coming into a station and, after glancing out of the window, he put out a hand and swiftly removed the Walkman from Lucy's ears.

Lucy woke, startled. A man's arm stretched out towards her; it was olive-skinned and hairy and there was one of those African elephant hair bracelets around his wrist. She guessed he was middle-aged by his voice, the throaty wheeze of a Gauloise addict, but couldn't be sure; his face was almost totally concealed beneath a broad-brimmed black hat.

'This is Siena,' the man was saying. 'Don't you want Siena?'

Lucy jumped up and looked quickly out of the window. She checked for the sign SIENA on the station platform and, grabbing her bag and her missing boot, leapt off the train without a backward glance.

But she could feel the man's presence as she crouched on the platform, pulling on her boot. He was there, as she'd suspected he would be, at the open window of the carriage, pointing his camera at her. 'What are you doing?'

'You remind me of someone,' he said in English spiced with a heavy Italian accent.

'What?' said Lucy. 'What on earth . . . ?'

'Hey,' said the man, 'I was on the plane with you.'

As though, Lucy thought, that explained everything. 'What?' she said. 'Shit.' She was too angry to be frightened and was just about to turn and stamp off towards the exit when the man spoke again.

'This is for you.' Snapping the cassette out of his camera he tossed it to her out of the window. It bounced off her and disappeared between the wheels of the train which was now moving slowly out of the station. Lucy waited until the train had gone and then looked down the track. There was

4

the cassette. She lowered herself over the edge of the platform.

Lucy sat in the back of the taxi being thrown from side to side as the driver negotiated the twists and turns of the Tuscan lanes with typical macho Italian verve. It was four years since she and her mother had driven through the hamlets and vine-covered hills to Diana and Ian Grayson's farmhouse. Lucy remembered the terrace outside the kitchen, with its large, companionable table which always seemed to be surrounded by old friends and new acquaintances eating and drinking and laughing. And she remembered her mother bursting into their bedroom before one of those evenings, wearing her silk flower-patterned kimono, running her fingers dramatically through her long, blonde hair and demanding hot water. 'Darling Lucy, how can I be expected to wash my hair without hot water?'

Lucy, who had been lying on her bed thinking of Niccolo and what had happened at the lake that afternoon, turned over idly: 'Why bother, Momma? Your hair looks fine to me.'

Her mother had tsked irritably. Being called Momma or Mummy or, indeed, anything that reminded her that she was old enough to have a teenage daughter, always annoyed her. 'Darling, in this heat I simply have to wash my hair. Can't you do something? Find someone to fix the plumbing. Get Diana . . .'

Lucy had uncoiled herself from the bed, padded

into the bathroom and run the tap. As her mother was exclaiming, 'I cannot imagine why my dearest friend should choose, willingly, to bury herself miles away from anywhere, without even the most basic civilised amenities . . .' the water had come gushing from the tap and the room had filled with steam. 'Darling,' her mother had murmured approvingly, 'you're so clever.'

'You just have to run the tap for a bit, that's all,' Lucy had said. She'd wondered then, as she wondered now, why she had always felt like the parent and never the child; why she'd always felt responsible for her beautiful, wayward mother. She just wished she'd been with her when it really mattered.

Lucy hadn't even known the anonymous man who had phoned in the middle of the night three years ago telling her father to get round to East 74th Street as soon as possible. 'There's been a terrible accident . . . your ex-wife. I've left the key with the janitor.' And when her father had arrived the man had disappeared without trace. There had been nobody there, her father had said, except Sarah . . . on the bed.

'*Americana?*' The taxi driver interrupted Lucy's memories.

'*Si,*' she replied. Her Italian was limited but adequate. At the beginning, when she'd first got back from Italy, she'd taken a few private Italian lessons with one of the College professors, but when Niccolo stopped writing to her there hadn't seemed much point in continuing.

She delved into her duffle for a packet of cigarettes and lit one. The taxi swerved around a corner, throwing her backwards.

'*Tutta sola?*' the driver gazed at her through his mirror, politely curious.

'*Si, si,*' Lucy said.

'*Non ha un marito?*'

'No,' Lucy said firmly.

'*Meglio sola,*' the driver said, nodding and smiling.

Lucy thought of Niccolo again and wasn't really absolutely sure that it was better to be alone. She dug back into her duffle and, this time, brought out a battered journal and a fibre pen. She'd cut out a picture, a detail of a fresco by Fra Filippo Lippi, and stuck it into the journal. It mirrored, almost exactly, in shades of green and ochre, the landscape outside the car window. Carefully she wrote next to the picture, 'I am not thinking of his face. . . Of what he wore or if he's tall. . . Or if he feels I've left a trace. . . I do not think of him at all.'

She gazed at the poem for a few moments and, although she was quite pleased with the way it sounded, she couldn't imagine what strange trick of the subconscious had summoned up those particular words. The truth was that there had scarcely been a day in the last four years when she hadn't thought about Niccolo Donati at least once. Ripping out the page, Lucy held it near the window and languidly watched the warm breeze carry it away across the hill.

In the distance she could just see, coming into

view, the Gothic splendour of the Castello Brolio across the valley from Diana and Ian's farmhouse. 'Look, darling,' her mother had murmured, impressed, during their last visit. 'Just look at that. We've wandered into a medieval film set.'

'*Momento*!' Lucy called out to the driver, pointing to a honey-coloured stone farmhouse high on a hill, with rolling countryside spread out around it. 'That's it. *La*. Over there.'

The taxi drove up the drive, deposited her and went off back down the lane in a cloud of red dust. She stood for a moment, holding her duffle, confronting the house. In the distance she could hear the hum of a tractor. Larger than life terracotta figures stood around in groups, lounged on the grass, sat on the terrace and peered into windows. They seemed to regard her beadily as she entered the courtyard leading up to the doorway. Lucy looked for a bell or a knocker and finding neither, walked through a glass door into Ian Grayson's studio. It was piled high with sketches, canvases, paints and giant blocks of wood, with finished and unfinished pieces of sculpture strewn about haphazardly. Lucy wandered around the room, feeling the wooden shapes with the palm of her hand and breathing in the evocative scent of turps, lavender and wood shavings.

Passing through another room filled with wine barrels and on into the living room, she saw a woman, who didn't look at all like the Diana she remembered, asleep on a sofa, snoring softly. Lucy quietly put down her duffle and her bag, helped

8

herself to a cherry from a wooden dish on a side table, and stepped out on to the terrace and into bright, dappled sunshine. In a hammock strung between two trees on the other side of the lawn lay an elderly man with a Panama hat over his face. She tiptoed past him to a *chaise longue* in the shade of a small awning. Lucy stood there, gazing at Diana indecisively. She gave a slight cough and when that elicited no response, hopefully rustled a couple of sketch pads on a nearby table. Diana – at least it looked like Diana, a pretty woman in her forties – slept on and Lucy, emboldened, took hold of an iron chair and scraped the legs on the flagstones. At last she looked up.

'Diana, Diana . . . hi,' Lucy said.

At first there was no recognition in Diana's eyes and then she suddenly sat up and flung her arms around Lucy.

'Lucy! Lucy! We were waiting for you to call. You didn't call, did you?'

'I took a cab.'

'Oh, my God, the soup.' Diana jumped to her feet and linked her arm in Lucy's, 'Come on in.' Hurrying her towards the kitchen, she called out to an upper window. 'Ian, wake up. Lucy's here.'

Lucy remembered the kitchen. Like something out of *House and Garden*: flagged floors, fruit and vegetables piled artistically in glossy wooden bowls and rustic, colourfully decorated, handmade furniture. 'The perfect backdrop for one of those cookery writers who's always doing clever things with basil,' her mother had said.

As Diana stirred and studied her soup, Lucy wandered over to the sideboard. Amongst the bric-à-brac was an erotic Indian miniature, rather beautiful, actually. Next to it stood a photograph of four generations of English women and a small bust of a bare-breasted girl.

'Ian did that – Miranda when she was thirteen,' Diana said, over her shoulder.

Lucy gazed at the bust curiously, and decided that when she was thirteen she probably wouldn't have liked to take off her clothes in front of her step-father.

'Tell me,' Diana was saying. 'How is your father . . . and his new wife?'

'He's okay,' Lucy said. 'They're trying to have another baby.' Her father had sent her on this trip because, he'd said, he wanted Ian to do a sculpture of her. Secretly, Lucy believed it was so that he and Maryanne could have some time alone together . . .

Their apartment, large by New York standards, had been fine for a single man and his young daughter; they'd both had their friends round, played their own kinds of music as loud as they liked and been able to chat endlessly on the phone without driving each other crazy. And then along had come pretty, well-meaning Maryanne (the recipient of most of her father's phone calls), followed, a respectable ten months later, by Jordan, and Jordan's daily nanny who always seemed to be in the kitchen boiling and sterilising things just when Maryanne was trying to fix dinner and Lucy had dashed in to get a Coke out of the refrigerator.

'Three women in a kitchen are two women too many,' her father would say jokily, anxious to defuse the tension.

Her father was good at joking and de-fusing tension. Goodness knows he'd had enough practice trying to control her mother's mood swings. Lucy sometimes wondered how he had the time to be a successful International Lawyer when he worried so much about the happiness of everyone around him. Was Maryanne missing her secretarial job at the ad agency? Was the nanny working too many hours? Was Lucy really enjoying college and why didn't she get out more and make new friends? She loved him very much. Perhaps that was why, in spite of her mother's confusing legacy, she still went right on thinking of him as her father. It had really shaken her, going through her mother's things after she'd died and finding that oblique poem, full of strange references to fighting and vineyards and Italy and the man she had met and loved there many years ago. Lucy hadn't understood it at first. But reading it and re-reading it, she had gradually become aware of the enormity of what it told her. Grant Harmon . . . Dad . . . was not her father. Lucy shifted uneasily. She still felt guilty about her reaction to this momentous discovery. For a while she'd felt like an orphan, desolate, deserted. And then, with scarcely a thought for Dad who'd loved and cared for her and been deceived, she'd begun to find it all rather exciting, spending hours speculating on the possible identity of her real father. A glamorously wicked freedom fighter?

A romantic literary figure? A member of the aristocracy? A Prince, even? Well, a Count, at the very least. . . Seeing Niccolo again was not the only reason she had so eagerly accepted the trip to Italy. She had come here to look for her father.

She hardly heard Diana when she said: 'You know, I had Daisy when I was forty.'

'Sorry . . .' Lucy collected her thoughts. 'I was miles away.'

Diana smiled at her. 'I didn't recognise you at first. I just can't get over how grown-up you look.'

'I hope so,' Lucy said, 'after four years.' She picked up a photograph of two young men: Diana's son and Niccolo Donati.

'Is Christopher here?'

Diana came across the room and looked over her shoulder, 'He was supposed to show up yesterday, for my birthday. For some reason it's become the one occasion when everyone descends on us. We've a full house at the moment. Usually it couldn't be quieter. But Christopher . . . well, he's still floating around Turkey somewhere with his friend Niccolo.'

'Niccolo Donati?'

'You remember him?'

Lucy nodded and quickly picked up another photo. It showed a chic woman in her twenties, wearing a bathing suit and sunglasses, *circa* nineteen seventy something. Except for the long, blonde hair she looked just like Lucy. 'Is this Connecticut? I remember that bathing suit.'

Diana took the picture, 'No. I took that in Forte dei Marmi.'

Lucy placed her hand over her mother's face. 'She always used to cut herself out of pictures.' Lacking a sense of self-worth; that's what the psychotherapist had said at the inquest. Lucy removed her hand and studied the woman laughing and waving at her out of the photograph. How could anyone so beautiful and talented not love herself?

'I still catch myself thinking I've got to ring her with some gossip,' Diana said. 'Not that I ever knew where she was. Even when she was here. What about those walks she used to take? Out she'd go and come back four hours later. "Nice walk?" I'd say. Once she said, "Too lovely for God."'

'I think she was kind of angry at God.'

'I suppose she was,' Diana said. 'I'd never have thought of that. Lucy, your mother had a very special ... well ... appetite for life. Probably too much of one.' Diana was choosing her words with care. 'It's what gave her work its ... dazzle.'

'Lucy, welcome.' Ian Grayson, dressed and refreshed from his nap, loped into the kitchen and hugged and kissed her awkwardly. 'Welcome, welcome.' After many years of exile there was still an agreeable Irish lilt to his voice. Lucy kissed him back warmly on both cheeks. She found Ian's craggy mixture of diffidence and arrogance reassuringly unthreatening. Last time she'd been here Ian and Diana had been grown-ups, her mother's friends. Now they seemed like people she could confide in, who might be able to help her.

'A little birthday torte, darling?' Diana nodded to

13

Ian, sliced the almond cake and put it on the table. 'And you, Lucy?'

They were about to sit down and devour the cake when an elegant woman, with long, auburn, curly hair, sauntered into the kitchen. 'I had a dream a family of homeless people were living in my closet,' she said, in an Italian accent, to the room at large. It was the woman who had been sleeping in the sitting room. She looked as if she were in her thirties but there was a sophistication about her that made Lucy suspect she must be nearer forty-five.

'Then somebody is getting some use out of that apartment at last,' Ian said, grinning at her. 'Lucy – Noemi.'

Noemi clasped Lucy's hand: 'Lucy, I knew your mother long ago. She once saved me from marrying a most unsuitable man.'

'She did?' Lucy said.

'She took him away with her to Venezia.' Noemi, with the confidence of a beautiful woman, was still holding Lucy's hand and her gaze, 'Your fingers are little ice cubes.'

Diana, who was now efficiently plucking a chicken, said: 'Was that the Count?'

'I don't think about it,' Noemi replied, smiling in what seemed to Lucy a rather lop-sided and sad manner. She dropped Lucy's hand and said in a determinedly cheerful voice, 'I gave up thinking about men altogether, remember?'

Diana laughed. 'Noemi writes a Lonely Hearts

14

column called *Ditelo a Noemi* – Tell Noemi. It has quite a following.'

Noemi went over the table, picked at the cake and made Mmm-ing noises of appreciation. 'Another culinary triumph, Diana. Oh, if only I was sensible enough to take my own advice.'

'Tell Diana,' Ian said. 'She's the one who sorts out everybody's problems around here.' He put an affectionate arm around his wife's shoulders and studied the chicken as she hacked off the head and feet. 'What are you making us?'

'God, I don't know,' Diana said. 'But I do know that someone's got to pick up the bread for dinner and I can't. And we need more wine. I don't know where Miranda's slunk off to, or Richard. I haven't seen anyone since lunch.'

'Can I help – do something?' Lucy offered. She wished she hadn't when Diana handed her the chicken's feet, head and entrails.

'Bung those in the bin.' Diana nodded towards a standing waste-bin where Lucy deposited the chicken bits. 'Thanks. Everyone pitches in here, Lucy. But don't worry, you've a few days before we really put you to work.'

'I was wondering . . .' Lucy said diffidently. 'My mother . . . when she was here originally . . . was there anyone special . . . I mean, a boyfriend?'

'And she's done her bit for today,' Ian said, ignoring the question. 'Come along, Lucy, I'll show you your room.' He retrieved her bags from the sitting room and led the way onto the terrace, then across the lawn.

15

Lucy looked around at the soft, rolling country-side and the terracotta figures, which already seemed as familiar as family friends. 'I remember this exactly, just from one week,' she said.

Ian gestured towards some grey boxes. 'My bees. If you don't bother them, they won't bother you.' He strode towards a stone cottage, just across from the house. 'See, we fixed up the old hay barn. It only took us twenty years. When we first came here there was nothing. No water, no heat. We didn't have a shilling. We spent every penny we had buying the place.'

He didn't add that funding the dodgy roof, the crumbling boundary walls, the antique plumbing, and all the other disasters lurking in an old house, sometimes seemed an intolerable burden, sapping his creativity and wearing down his naturally passionate and optimistic nature.

Lucy looked at him curiously. 'Why did you move here?'

'To work. There's a great tradition of art in these hills. It's also not too hard on the eyes, or the nerves.'

'Last time,' said Lucy, 'we stayed in a room with some chimes.'

'Miranda's,' said Ian.

'Mummy hated them. She wrapped them in a scarf.'

Ian laughed. 'Yes. That sounds like Sarah the insomniac.' They walked passed an open doorway revealing a bedroom with medicines on the table and an unmade bed, and then Ian led Lucy into a large, loft-like room, full of pictures, sculptures and individual pieces of furniture hand made from glossy dark wood. 'Here we are. This is you.'

Lucy, wandering about, touching this and that, pulled aside a curtain to reveal, on the other side, a wash-basin, bidet and a handsomely painted dark green Victorian bath, standing on claw feet. The romantic room perfectly matched her mood.

Ian dropped Lucy's duffle and bag and opened a shuttered window. 'Next door you've got Alex Parish. Old friend of ours . . . he knew your mother, too. He's been very sick. It's sad, disturbing for all of us.'

'The playwright?' Lucy was intrigued. 'He's sick?'

'You know him? said Ian. 'Smart girl.'

'We had him in playwriting class,' Lucy said.

'Alex . . . being read in college?' Ian chuckled: 'He'll be thrilled. So, you want to be a writer like your mother?'

'No. . . I mean, I write in a journal, sort of, but I wouldn't call it being a writer.' Lucy looked around for Ian who was circling her, studying her.

He was looking at her with a professional's eye – the soft curve of a cheek, the full red lips which owed nothing to cosmetics – but also with lingering appreciation, the way any man looks at a lovely woman.

'I did her portrait once, you know,' he said.

'I know.' Lucy wished he'd stop gazing at her like that. 'My father has it at home. It's beautiful.'

'I hope you're patient, because I fumble along. You'll help?'

17

'How?'

'Let me look at you,' Ian said, still looking ... admiring.

'Not all the time, I hope.'

'You won't even be aware,' Ian said confidently. 'So. Get settled, take a swim. We eat at sunset, but come up before.'

After Ian had left, Lucy pulled at the window shade which, with some difficulty, opened on to a wide view. Lucy knew that villa on the next hill. She was still staring at it, some minutes later, when a noise disturbed her. Looking down she saw, below her, a thin man in a wheelchair, attached to an intravenous drip. He was bending forward, grimacing in pain. His rather dashing knitted helmet shifted slightly as he moved, and, underneath, his hair was unnaturally thin. He looked old but Lucy could see that he wasn't old at all, probably in his fifties, just terribly ill. This must be Alex Parish, the playwright. There was spit slipping from his mouth. Lucy watched as, with considerable effort, he raised his head and aimed the spit at an ant scrabbling in a pile of dirt.

Feeling a bit like a voyeur, she withdrew from the window, went over to her duffle, fished through it and took out a small knapsack. Inside it was her journal. She flipped through the pages. It was full of scrapbook bits and pieces, and pictures of her mother, including one in a long white dress and another torn from a fashion magazine, showing her modelling the sort of conventionally cut county tweeds she would never have chosen to wear.

18

Eventually, Lucy found what she was looking for. From a taped-in envelope she carefully extracted a faded Polaroid of herself and Niccolo Donati, sitting close together next to a stone pillar, alongside steps leading down to a lake. Lucy sat down on the bed, looked at the snapshot for several minutes and then slipped it under her shirt, over her heart.

CHAPTER TWO

After a bit of desultory unpacking, Lucy put on her swimsuit and a baggy shirt and went in search of the swimming pool. She had just stubbed out her cigarette in one of the cavities of the ancient, pinkish-brown, crumbling wall beneath the terrace, when a slipper fell at her feet like a reproach. It was the sort of velvet slipper, with an embroidered gold crest on the front, that very old people get given at Christmases and birthdays when nobody can think what else to give them. She started guiltily and looked up. On the terrace was the same elderly gentleman she'd seen in the hammock, still wearing his Panama hat.

'Is this your slipper?'

'I suppose so.' He lifted his hat courteously. 'Do I know you?'

'I'm Lucy ... Lucy Harmon.'

'And I am Guillaume. *Enchanté.* Here for a visit?'

'Ian's doing a sculpture of me,' said Lucy. 'Diana was a friend of my mother's.'

Monsieur Guillaume wagged a warning finger. 'Aha, watch. Ian's an Indian piper, charming form out of his material.'

Lucy was squinting against the sun as she looked up at the old man, shielding her eyes with her hand. 'It's sort of an excuse for my father to send me to Italy – as a present.'

'Which indeed it is.' Monsieur Guillaume who, due to his great age, was only rarely addressed as Guy by the Graysons and their friends, looked around distractedly. 'But where is Signor Bruno? He was to help me repair my bed. A man needs a bed on which to dream, doesn't he?'

'If he dreams,' Lucy said.

'Everyone dreams. Many just don't remember. The saints used to call them visions, you know. Giotto's San Francesco is merely having nightmares. But a pretty girl should not sleep with nightmares . . .' He gently touched the lines around his eyes, '. . . it wrinkles the sheets.'

'I'll remember that,' Lucy said. Monsieur Guillaume started to withdraw and she flung his slipper up onto the terrace. 'Hey, your slipper.'

He picked it up and examined it curiously. 'Oh . . . *merci, Mademoiselle. Merci . . .*'

Lucy told him that she was going for a swim and the old man thanked her again and went off along the terrace, muttering to himself about the elusive Signor Bruno. Behind him Lucy caught sight of Ian, standing in the doorway of his studio watching them. She shrugged, she was getting used to people staring at her.

The pool was at the end of a long vineyard. It wasn't a glossy, tiled affair with dolphins spouting water like the one they used to go to in Connecticut; more of a large cement tub edged with old stonework and sunk into the field. Now, it was bathed in the soft pink of a sensational sunset, and the idyllic impression was completed by the young, naked woman lying asleep beside the pool, only partially draped in a towel.

Lucy took off her shirt and, in her black one-piece swimsuit, slipped quietly into the water. Breaking the surface as smoothly as a trout, she dived adeptly to the bottom where she could see a small drop earring. She retrieved it and, gliding upwards to deposit the jewel at the side of the pool, came face to face with the naked girl.

'Jesus,' the girl said, looking down at Lucy. 'I thought you were drowning. I was wondering whether I was going to have to leap in and save you or something.'

Lucy hauled herself out. 'Are you Miranda?'

'Yes,' Miranda said. 'God, I can't stop sleeping, it's the air, I guess. You were here before, weren't you?'

'Four years ago.' Lucy retrieved her towel and rubbed her hair. 'Your brother was here, not you.'

'I don't really live in Tuscany,' said Miranda, 'although Christopher and I spent a lot of time here when Mummy and Ian got together.'

'How old were you when . . . well, when they got together?' said Lucy.

'About eight, I suppose,' Miranda said, 'and Chris is a few years younger. We were both born in Madison, New Jersey – suburban USA – which is probably why we now choose to live in New York.'

'Me, too,' Lucy said. 'I mean, that's where I live.'

'It's where it all happens, isn't it?' Miranda said.

'But we come every year for Mummy's birthday. To console her. Unfortunately, Christopher doesn't seem capable of finding his way out of Turkey.'

'He's with Niccolo?'

Miranda nodded. 'You know Niccolo?'

'From last time—'

Miranda interrupted: 'You don't smoke by any miracle, do you?'

'Not really,' Lucy lied, only too aware of the average New Yorker's evangelical attitude towards cigarettes.

'Richard freaks out when I smoke,' Miranda said. 'Do you go to college in New York?'

'My first year . . .' Lucy gazed around at the fields. 'These are all grape vines?'

'They are.' From the other side of the stone wall, a farmer on his tractor was smiling at them appreciatively. Miranda swiftly wrapped herself in her towel and waved towards him, gold bracelets jangling glamorously on her wrists, '*Ciao*, Signor Bruno!' She turned back to Lucy. 'Mummy and Ian tried to sell it a while back but it was a financial disaster.'

'When are they coming back?' Lucy said.

'Who?'

'Your brother.'

'Who knows . . .' Miranda shrugged. 'They said—' She stopped suddenly and waved at a man who was jogging towards them, dressed in a navy and white tracksuit teamed with unnaturally clean white Reeboks.

'Hi, babe.' He came up to them and stood there,

jogging on the spot in what Lucy considered a rather irritating manner. He looked at her, questioningly.

'It's ... ah ... you know ... Harmon ... Mummy's friend's daughter,' Miranda said, embarrassed.

'Lucy,' said Lucy.

'Right – Lucy.'

'God, Sarah Harmon's daughter?' Richard said in a voice which managed to be ingratiating and booming at the same time. 'Your mother was a great poet.' He shook Lucy's hand and gazed sincerely into her eyes. 'Richard Reed and I'm honoured to meet you.'

'It was my mother, not me,' Lucy said.

'Your mother made me want to be a poet once.' Richard bent down and unlaced his trainers. 'You know, I think it would be wonderful just to sit around all day and express yourself.'

Miranda seemed surprised. 'Richard, I didn't know you wrote poetry.'

'Never did, hon'. Don't have a creative bone in my body. It just seemed like a great idea at the time.' He took off his tracksuit top, breathed deeply as though he'd just discovered fresh air and flexed his muscles in Lucy's direction. 'You know why I became an entertainment lawyer? So I could be around creative people – like Miranda.'

Lucy looked at Miranda who said, with genuine modesty: 'I design jewellery. I'm apprenticed to this real asshole in New York who is, actually, a genius.'

24

Lucy picked up the earring and handed it to Miranda. 'Is this one of yours?'

'Yes, but that's old shit.' Miranda casually chucked the earring back into the pool and ran a hand seductively down Richard's naked spine. 'Are you going in?'

'What's it like, Lucy?' Richard nodded towards the pool.

'Quiet as a tomb,' Lucy said and gazed firmly at the vineyard as Richard pulled off his tracksuit bottom and his minuscule white underpants, and dived in.

There was a lot of gossip, about local personalities and politics Lucy didn't understand, over a deliciously simple dinner of soup, roast chicken, grilled peppers, fruit and cheese. Afterwards, Monsieur Guillaume went to bed and Noemi, with minimal help from Ian, tackled the washing up. Miranda and Richard put on a Billie Holiday tape in the sitting room and swayed about, as if welded together: her arm tightly around his neck, his hands firmly cupping the shiny black silk dress tightly outlining her thighs. Every now and again they paused, closed their eyes, and kissed enthusiastically. Lucy noticed that Alex Parish was sitting quietly in a corner watching them and sipping something she later discovered to be the liquid morphine which kept him going.

Diana nodded to her. 'Come on, Lucy, I want to show you something.' She led the way into the study and, delving into an old oak chest, brought out a long, silk chiffon patterned white dress. 'After your mother got married she said she was going to be fat and happy and she'd have no more use for it. Of course she never gained an ounce.' Diana held up the dress and studied it regretfully. 'I could never carry it off.'

Lucy gazed at the dress in amazement. 'I don't believe it. I've just been looking at a picture of Mom in that very dress.'

Diana handed it to Lucy. 'Come on, slip it on . . . it's so pretty. Arms through here . . . that's it. You can wear it to the Donatis' party. They give a lovely one every summer.'

Lucy smoothed the dress over her breasts and hips and, when she turned to show Diana, the skirt of diagonally tiered frills flounced out around her long, slender legs.

Diana stood back and looked at her sombrely, as though encountering a ghost. 'You know, you could be Sarah, twenty years ago, coming to help me fix up this place.'

Lucy laughed disbelievingly. '*She* helped you fix it up?'

Diana giggled, 'Well . . . with a lot of hash breaks. Look, jump up on that chair. The dress is a little long, that's all.' She reached over to the table for a box of pins. 'I hope you don't hate her,' she said, her eyes on the pinning. 'We all have to hate our parents a little, but not too much. Your mother needed to take risks, you know.' She continued to concentrate on the hem for a while and then said

26

slowly, almost as though she was trying to convince herself, 'That kind of person ends up hurting others, I think, without meaning to.'

'I don't think she really noticed,' Lucy said.

'Oh, Lucy, she did. I think it's why she hurt herself the most.' Diana was working around the back now. 'But I admired that recklessness in her. It's so . . . not me. I thought it brave. I couldn't live the way she did. I'm not the type. Neither is Ian.' She sat back on her heels and, twirling Lucy around to face her, checked the hem-length and then looked up. 'You know, we've been faithful to each other for twenty years. Can you believe that?'

'Yes,' Lucy said.

'Most people can't. But I count on it. It's something which actually matters a lot to me.'

Lucy felt that Diana was telling her something terribly important and she wished she knew what it was. Eventually she said: 'I can see that.'

'Yes, but you're not an old lady like me,' said Diana. 'Your illusions haven't been stolen away.'

Diana put the unused pins neatly away in the sewing box and carried it and Sarah Harmon's dress into the bedroom where Ian was lying in bed reading the latest Dick Francis paperback. She undressed, put on a cotton nightdress and started brushing her hair.

Ian looked up from his book. 'Have you noticed, she walks the exact same way?'

'And the expression,' Diana said, 'it's too . . .'

'Well, I think it's very strange of this father of

27

hers. He never cared for my work; he didn't like the portrait I did of Sarah. Why does he suddenly want Lucy to come here?'

'Maybe it was Lucy who wanted to come here.'

'Why does it feel so annoying?'

'Ian, he's rich and is kindly throwing money our way.'

'It is a commission, Diana,' Ian said coldly. 'You make it sound like charity.'

Diana got up and busied herself folding clothes and hanging garments in the cupboard. 'Sweet, I'm sure he's mad about your work. I'm just happy we can get the roof fixed. Poor Lucy, stranded with us old fogeys . . .'

'Speak for yourself.'

'I'm sure she'd rather be out chasing boys around somewhere on a beach.'

'She seemed rather serious to me.'

'Or being chased.' Diana put on a towelling robe. 'At nineteen it's all about boys. I caught her looking at a picture of Christopher.'

'Ha, Christopher,' Ian said.

Diana picked up the sewing basket and the dress. 'Why not?' she said, sounding defensive. 'She's nineteen.'

'And thinking about boys,' Ian agreed equably. He had no intention of getting into the familiar pointless discussion about Christopher's debatable sexuality. Diana appeared to be going off with her sewing things. 'Not sleepy?' he said.

'No. Not at all. I've got to finish Daisy's dress, and

I might just put up Lucy's hem, too.' She stood in the doorway. 'I won't wake you when I come in.'

Ian put down his book and said gruffly, 'Come here.' Diana came back to the bed. 'Goodnight kiss?' Diana was surprised but she bent and kissed Ian's eyebrow, anyway. 'Is that all?' he said. Diana kissed him lightly on the mouth. He watched her as she walked away from him. 'You were nineteen once, I suppose, weren't you?'

Diana felt bruised by the question. 'I suppose I must have been.' She shut the bedroom door quietly behind her and went down the hall into the dark living room.

She didn't turn on the light, but put down her sewing box, sat down on the sofa and gazed into space.

Diana had been nineteen, in her first year at Trinity College, Dublin, when Simon Schermer from Madison, New Jersey had strolled into the Buttery and into her life – a glamorous older man amongst all the students with their tubes of Clearasil and tins of Nescafé. He was twenty-seven and doing a postgraduate degree in Theoretical Physics and Pure Mathematics. That alone should have alerted her to the fact that they had absolutely nothing in common. He spent his time gazing in fascinated wonder at algebraic hieroglyphics and she was forever reading – a legitimate pastime, since her subjects were English Literature and History of Art and Architecture. She never got the degree, though; she left the following year, having conceived Miranda and married Simon Schermer instead.

Diana remembered phoning up her old schoolfriend, Sarah, to relay the news that she was having a baby and was about to marry the father – an American who looked just like Montgomery Clift.

Instead of whooping with pleasure and congratulations as Diana had hoped she might, Sarah had lectured her bossily about the safety net of having a good degree under your belt rather than a baby. 'Do you want to lose your freedom for ever?' she'd said. 'Take my advice and get rid of it. Even if the guy looks like Cary Grant.'

Diana had put the phone down, then. And they hadn't spoken again until Miranda was four years old. Diana had been stuck in Madison, with a toddler and Christopher, the new baby, and Sarah had paid them a fleeting visit, bringing with her the scent of patchouli and an exciting world beyond *Sesame Street*. She'd been in New York doing a catwalk show for Halston, and had taken the commuter train out one evening, staying overnight.

It was not a wild success. They sat on the lawn drinking double Martinis and were massacred by mosquitoes. 'I'm going to look just great in the wedding dress tomorrow,' Sarah had said. 'Thank God there's a veil.' And, when they went inside to escape the insects, Simon asked her not to smoke. 'We have babies in this house, Sarah, who have to be protected against pollutants.'

Simon left very early the following morning, to do something Diana never really quite understood in Corporate Finance, and Sarah lit up a Marlborough and looked at Diana quizzically over the breakfast table. 'And does he look that bad-tempered and sulky all the time? Like Montgomery Clift?'

'Of course not,' Diana told her, but she was lying. Simon's habitual expression, which had once seemed to her so sultry and sexy was, in fact, an indication of ill humour. He rarely laughed and always seemed cross about something. Diana, driving Miranda to pre-playschool or sweeping leaves off the lawn (the neighbours complained if she didn't) often wondered guiltily if it was because he felt trapped by her and the babies.

No wonder that after him she'd fallen in love with Ian, a boisterous Irishman who laughed a lot. Ian was not neat and precise or worried about why his sock drawer was full of mis-matches. Diana had been pretty sure he didn't even have a sock drawer. But he did have designer stubble long before art directors decided it was chic not to shave and he looked nothing at all like Montgomery Clift.

They'd met at the Royal Academy. Simon's firm had sent him over to England to run the London office, and Diana had needed to get some pictures framed for the new house in Weybridge. She was in the Framing Department around the back of the Academy when Ian came in with some frames he'd been commissioned to make for them.

'That's the one I want,' she'd said to the

assistant, pointing to an elaborately carved oak frame under Ian's arm.

'Is it me you're after?' Ian had said, grinning at her.

And, as it turned out, it was.

Months later they decided that they couldn't live without each other and Diana had extricated herself from her marriage. It hadn't been as agonising as she'd expected. Simon turned out to have been enjoying, for the past year, a highly unprofessional relationship with Paula, his P.A., a nice woman who didn't care too much about laughter and actively wanted to live in an Executive Home in Weybridge, Surrey or Madison, New Jersey.

Ian had no emotional entanglements. For some reason Diana couldn't fathom, and for whch she would always be grateful, he had reached the age of thirty-five without ever getting around to marrying any of the women he'd loved, including the ones who had yearned to become Mrs Grayson. He sold his studio in Clerkenwell ('To include commodious living accommodation on the first floor . . .') and made just enough on the deal to buy the broken down farmhouse he and Diana had coveted when they'd discovered it during one illicit, idyllic Tuscan weekend.

Sarah had approved of Ian as fervently as she'd disapproved of Simon. 'He's got the soul of a true Celt,' she'd said. 'It's the Irish in you that finds him irresistible.'

And yet, Diana thought, she'd never come back – not after that first time. Not until four years ago when she'd brought Lucy to see them. Diana had felt sorry for Lucy, then. She'd been unnaturally quiet for a fifteen-year-old. Constantly ministering to her mother's needs, she had seemed to exist only as Sarah's quiescent shadow. But towards the end of their stay she'd suddenly blossomed, giving a glimpse of the beauty she had now become.

Diana looked out of the window towards the cottage. She could just see Lucy, leaning on her windowsill, smoking and writing. It could have been Sarah. . . Sighing and returning to the present Diana turned her head away, put on the light and opened her sewing box.

Lucy lit a candle and a joint and, taking them both over to the window, gazed reflectively at the house. She was thinking about her mother's poem, which she kept secreted in her journal. After a while she picked up the book and wrote: 'I have her secret deep within. . . For years I've had to hide. . . I've brought the clues and now I'm here. . . To bring the truth outside.'

Reading it through it sounded a bit trite, not nearly important enough for how she felt. She ripped out the page and held it in the flame of the candle until it disintegrated into ash.

Brushing the ash off the long T-shirt she wore for bed and snuffing out the joint, Lucy caught sight of her reflection in the floor-length mirror. She ran her hands down the T-shirt, assessing her breasts as objectively as she had just assessed her poem. Neither, she felt, were up to her mother's standard.

There had been many times, particularly when she'd got low grades in English or when some guy she'd fancied had failed to follow up an initial date, that Lucy had considered it very unfair to have as a mother not just an internationally famous model, but a poet the *New York Times* had once compared with Sylvia Plath. How could she possibly live up to that? It was standard for any boy she brought home to fall in love with her mother and later, when Lucy had been around sixteen, for them to react the way Richard Reed had done that afternoon. 'Wow! Is your mother really *the* Sarah Harmon?' But, of course, they never experienced her mother's manic depressive moods. It was only since she'd died that Lucy had begun to understand why her mother had been so stressed out. She, too, had always had something to live up to – her reputation as a beauty and a writer. Lucy had known it was no good competing; she'd comforted herself with the knowledge that, unlike her mother, she could change a plug, make an omelette souffle, and write a coherent laundry list.

Lucy climbed into bed and shut her eyes but was unable to sleep. Through the wall she could hear Alex Parish coughing. But it wasn't the coughing that was keeping her awake, only disturbing thoughts of Niccolo. It was Niccolo who had made her feel, for the first time, desirable and beautiful. He hadn't gone overboard about her mother, either. 'She laughs a lot, your mother,' he'd said as they'd walked through the vineyard, 'but the laughter is not in her eyes.'

Lucy turned restlessly, again and again. Eventually, exasperated, she swung her legs down onto the kelim rug, slid onto the floor and, pulling her T-shirt over her knees, rolled over pressing her lips and cheeks to the cold floor in frustrated longing. Suddenly, the door creaked. She sat bolt upright as it slowly opened to reveal Alex Parish standing in the doorway, his emaciated body lost in a pair of striped pyjamas and a loose cotton dressing gown.

'Please excuse me, but you wouldn't happen to have any more of that interesting brand of cigarette I can smell?'

'Hi. Hang on a minute.' She put on a robe and retrieving the joint and a box of matches, said, 'I'll join you outside.' She spread the kelim rug down on the grass under the stars. She was intrigued by actually meeting Alex Parish, and rather flattered that he had sought her out. 'Will this be okay for you?'

Alex gave a twisted smile. 'Thank you. I can still manage to sit down.'

But Lucy saw that he managed it only with difficulty. She sat down next to him, re-lit the joint and passed it to him. 'We did *The Lost Lover* in college last term,' she said. She'd been around writers long enough to know that they liked nothing better than talking about their work.

Alex tried not to look pleased. 'It's not my best play, but it's the one they'll put on my tombstone.'

'I like the part where everyone freezes,' Lucy said. 'It really shows how much grief he has.'

Alex looked at Lucy, not hearing her, not really

seeing her. 'She was larger than life, your mother. She radiated . . . I don't know . . . not like the sun, more like the moon.'

'What? Reflected light?'

'No,' Alex said thoughtfully. 'Luminous. . . And, I imagine, difficult to have as a mother.'

'I didn't see her much after they got divorced,' Lucy said truthfully. She'd been twelve when her parents had split up and she'd known it was going to happen almost before they did. Her mother's temperament had been so combustible that, in spite of her father's soothing efforts, it sometimes seemed the apartment would explode with repressed tension and resentment.

It was her father who had told her, of course. Her mother couldn't face up to it. Later she'd put her arms around Lucy and wept: 'Darling Lucy, Daddy and I both think it's better for you to stay here, with him.' She'd wiped away the tears then and added with false gaiety, 'You know me, darling, out and about, here and there. Daddy can give you the stability and security you need; and you'll be able to stay on at school . . . all your friends, and so on . . .'

'There was never anyone like your mother,' Alex said. 'I don't suppose there were a lot of models scribbling transporting little verses in between fashion shoots.'

Lucy wrapped her arms around her knees and gazed at Alex with interest. 'When did you know her?'

'Way back,' said Alex, passing her the joint.

36

Lucy felt a flicker of hope. She genuinely admired Alex as a playwright and she liked the wry way he smiled at her, as though they were equal, old friends. 'Were you a boyfriend of hers?'

'I wouldn't say that,' Alex said. 'I probably tried.'

Lucy persisted. 'Do you remember her having a pair of green sandals?'

Alex looked perplexed. 'Shoes?'

'No,' said Lucy. 'Sandals.'

Alex laughed. 'I can't say I do.' He noticed that Lucy was smoking the joint through her fist: 'I'm not contagious, you know.'

It was the one thing Lucy disliked about pot – being passed somebody else's lip-moistened joint; it was even more off-putting then being at the end of the line in front of the altar when the communion cup came round. 'I always smoke it this way with people,' she said, passing it back to him.

Alex drew deeply and gratefully on the grass. He gazed out towards the house. There was a light on in the sitting room, another in one of the upstairs rooms. People leading their lives, with time left to live them.

'One doctor told me three months,' he said. 'He, of course, is the most expensive doctor. One said a week or two, depending on my luck. According to another, I shouldn't be here at all.'

Lucy was stricken, for Alex and for herself. If Alex was potentially her father, as she was beginning to hope, she would have found him only to lose him again. 'That's awful.'

'Worse with reactions like that,' Alex said sharply.

'What reaction would you like?'

'Lies.' Alex was beginning to feel stoned. 'Truth is no longer interesting to me . . . unless it's a secret. Secrets are always interesting.'

'I'm sorry,' Lucy smiled. 'I don't have a secret for you.'

'No?' Alex looked at her curiously. 'What about boys? There must be someone you're mad about.'

Lucy blushed. 'No one very.'

'Come on,' said Alex. 'Who's the Superman back home?'

'There is no Superman back home,' Lucy said firmly.

'Oh, so he's an aesthete.'

'There isn't . . .' Lucy was beginning to resent this intrusive line of questioning. 'Why should I have a boyfriend?'

'Sorry, sorry.' Alex put his hands in the air placatingly. 'You're a beautiful girl . . . your mother had lots of boyfriends.'

'That was my mother,' Lucy said.

'I just meant. . . Listen . . . it's not as if I'd know for long.'

Lucy was instantly contrite. She supposed that when you were really ill – well, dying – the only thing left to be interested in was somebody else's future. 'I liked this boy,' she said hesitantly. 'I met him one summer when I was fifteen. He was the first person I really kissed.'

'Come on, come on,' Alex encouraged.

'Well, we wrote each other for a while. There was this one letter that was, I thought, so absolutely incredible . . .' Talking about it, Lucy discovered, made it all seem real, not just two people in a frozen snapshot. 'About there being an animal prowling through his heart. I memorised it completely. Anyway,' she said with brave honesty, 'after a while he stopped writing.'

'And no sex?' Alex queried. 'I always think that the only thing better than sex . . . maybe . . . is good pot.'

'I wouldn't know,' Lucy said. 'I haven't really had it that much.'

'Pot?'

'No,' Lucy smiled, 'sex.'

'You mean you've *never* slept with anyone?' Alex looked at her incredulously. 'That's a pretty good secret.'

'I slept in the same bed with my friend's brother once,' Lucy said. 'But we kept all our clothes on.'

They both started laughing, falling against each other, agreeably stoned.

Alex put an arm around Lucy's shoulders. 'I can understand it. The shock of losing someone when you're young . . . you stop developing.'

'It's not because of my mother,' Lucy said, drawing away from him. 'It's not.' Why did every conversation, every glance seem to lead back to her mother? 'Who do you see who's together and still happy? Not one of my friends' parents are still married to each other.'

'Mine were,' Alex said gloomily. 'The problem of

39

my life has been not being able to achieve the same thing. Either way you're lost.'

'Perhaps it's easier to stay alone,' Lucy said.

Alex turned to her. 'Lucy, Lucy, Lucy ... you can't have decided that at your age. You know what I think? You're in need of a ravisher.'

'I haven't completely decided,' Lucy said uneasily. 'I'm just ...'

'What?'

'Waiting.'

'Lucy, Lucy, Lucy ...'

Lucy shook her head crossly. 'Oh, do stop saying that.'

'You're scared. But there's something else ...' Alex studied Lucy's face. 'I can see ... you seem to be—'

'Stoned,' said Lucy who didn't want him to start psychoanalysing her again. She got up. 'I'm going to bed.'

'Wait ...' Alex reached for her wrist, brushed his lips along the back of her hand, breathing in the scent of her and experiencing the unexpected pang of something he was surprised to identify as lust. 'Sweet dreams.'

In the distance Diana sat watching them.

CHAPTER THREE

Diana cherished the quiet moments before breakfast, when she was alone on the terrace and the house and its environs were beginning to stir with familiar early morning noises. Pipes clanked, windows opened and shut, and in the distance she could hear a cock crowing and one of the Donatis' dogs barking; judging by this morning's high-pitched tone he had either spotted a passing rabbit or the postman.

She spread a yellow and white linen cloth on the terrace table and haphazardly laid out yellow plates and mugs. The sun was climbing high above the horizon, promising another hot, hazy day. Diana had never told Ian – she'd hate him to think she was criticising the home he'd made for them here – how often she longed for a stray cloud or a spot of rain to sully the ceaseless sunshine. How she would welcome the chance to look up at the sky, and wonder how the day would turn out. She knew all too well how today would turn out; like yesterday, the day before and the week before that. The sun would blaze down and she'd be forced into the shower by midday and totally exhausted if she didn't manage to fit in an after-lunch siesta.

God, I'm an ungrateful bitch, she said to herself

as she strolled down through the vines to pick fresh grapes and figs for the breakfast table. This pleasant ritual always soothed and delighted her; so much more satisfying than queueing and paying at the supermercato. She filled her basket and, returning to the terrace, saw Noemi coming out of the house carrying a terracotta butter dish and stone jars of home-made apricot jam and fresh honey.

She smiled at Noemi gratefully. Noemi was one of the few house guests who did what was needed instinctively instead of asking if there was anything they could do. 'Bless you, Noemi,' she said and, following her back into the kitchen, decanted the grapes and figs from her wicker basket into one of Ian's carved elm bowls. Setting it on the table, she looked up to see Alex limping towards her, leaning heavily on a cane. 'Look who's up and about,' she said in surprise.

'I had a great night.' Alex sat down cautiously, propping his cane against the chair.

Diana recalled the scene she had witnessed the previous evening. 'You met Lucy?'

'She's irresistible. I'm mad about her,' said Alex. 'Look, Monsieur Guillaume is busy already.'

Diana waved to the old man, who was meticulously watering the plants in the urns and around the base of the pergola, and came and sat down next to Alex. 'Now, what's that smile about?'

'What smile?'

'Come on, tell.'

'There's nothing to tell. I mean, we just talked.'

'What did she tell you?'

'I have a feeling, not as much as she might have done.'

'Oh, come on . . .'

Alex shook his head, 'No, no, no. You can't keep a secret.'

'Of course I can.' Diana nudged him.

'Really?'

'Yes, really. Lately I've been learning how. I've been practising.'

'What's going on?' said Noemi, coming out with a loaded breakfast tray.

'Nothing's going on,' Alex said.

Diana took the coffee pot and milk jug from the tray and began pouring. 'Noemi what would you tell your readers about a man who dangles a secret in front of you?'

'I wasn't dangling,' Alex protested, laughing.

'Oh, yes, you were . . .'

'No, I wasn't . . .'

'He wants to tell it.' Noemi sat down, put her elbows on the table, took a sip of coffee and smiled encouragingly at Alex over the top of her mug. '*Ditelo a Noemi*,' she said.

Lucy awoke and looked at her clock. It was past ten o'clock. She washed hastily, flung on a shirt and a pair of shorts and hurried out onto the terrace. Everyone was there, chattering animatedly, but they fell silent as she approached the table. Lucy thought she heard a murmured 'sssh'.

'My time's all screwed up,' she said. 'Sorry.'

'Time . . .' Diana said, pulling out a chair, 'we

don't even think about it here.' She passed Lucy some bread and a bowl of tomatoes. 'Here, rub some tomato on your bread, it's a very Tuscan thing to do.'

Lucy sat down, took the tomato and tentatively rubbed it on a chunk of ciabatta. Everyone seemed to be watching her. Not, Lucy thought, as though they were interested in seeing how she tackled this interesting Italian snack, but in an oddly embarrassing sort of way.

Miranda, studying Lucy reflectively, broke the silence. 'We're going to have to find Lucy some friends so she won't get bored with us old people.'

Noemi reached for the honey. 'Please, please don't say that, darling. If you're an old person, what does that make me?'

'Ageless,' Alex said, with a gallant half bow.

Noemi smiled at him and Miranda continued as though neither of them had spoken, 'How about Filippo Castellini? He's cute.'

Lucy glanced accusingly at Alex, realising that he must have regaled the group with their previous night's conversation. He was careful to avoid her gaze.

'Too perverse for an American girl,' Noemi said.

'Noemi,' Alex said, 'would you pass me some sugar?' From the tone of his voice he might just as well have said, Noemi, would you please shut up.

'How about Harry Fenimore-Jones?' Miranda offered.

'You don't mean that guy at dinner the other night?' said Richard. 'He was a complete idiot.'

Lucy swallowed a large piece of bread and said: 'That's okay. You don't need to find me any—'

She was interrupted by M. Guillaume, drifting past with his watering can. 'Won't Christopher and Niccolo be back soon?'

Lucy looked at Diana expectantly, but before she could reply a phone rang, unexpectedly close. Richard picked up the cellular phone by his plate and left the table, shouting in an unnecessarily loud voice: 'Hiya. What time is it over there?'

'Niccolo . . .' Miranda said. 'Now there's an idea . . .'

'Not Niccolo,' said Noemi. 'He's a terrible flirt. Watch out for him, Lucy.'

Alex picked up the fleeting expression of unease in Lucy's face as Diana said, 'Lucy knows him.'

'Well then, what about Carter Clay?' said Miranda.

Alex leaned over in front of Miranda and took the sugar bowl. 'Do you take sugar, Lucy?'

Diana shot Miranda a warning look. 'Okay, Miranda, enough.'

Miranda had long ago refused to acknowledge her mother's meaningful looks. 'Yes,' she said triumphantly, 'Carter Clay would love Lucy.'

'Stop it,' Diana cried. 'Leave her alone. She just got here.'

'I feel like a walking Lonely Hearts ad,' Lucy said, biting into another great hunk of bread and wishing she could disappear behind it.

At the sound of a distant bulldozer Alex, eager to divert everyone's attention, struggled gratefully to his feet. 'There it goes again. Come and see, Lucy, what we've got to put up with here.' He picked up his cane and hobbled over to the far edge of the terrace, followed by the rest of the group. 'The noise. You might as well be in downtown Manhattan.'

In the background they could hear Richard down on the lawn, shouting into his cellular phone: 'Can't find any decent mustard, otherwise the food's pretty good. No, I've hardly left the hotel. Yeah ... like a dog. Listen, gotta go now, the Japanese will be here any minute ...' He shoved the aerial back into his phone with a brisk, executive gesture and strode over to the others, who were gazing across the valley at the building construction getting under way on the opposite hill.

'What is it?' Lucy said.

'A *repetitore*,' said Noemi.

'They're building a TV mast,' said Alex.

'For brainwashing the Italian electorate,' Diana added.

'You don't like it,' said Miranda, 'because it messes up your view.'

Monsieur Guillaume stepped forward. 'It's a disgrace. Signor Bruno, next door, has been forced to sell them part of his land.' He started angrily waving his watering can in the direction of the bulldozers, slurping out water and shouting: 'Bastards! Philistines! Shits!'

Everyone clapped him enthusiastically.

'Bravo!'

46

'Bravissimo!'

'Get 'em!'

'More . . . more!'

'You should take them to court,' Richard said.

'Can't sue the government, Richard.' Diana's anxious gaze softened as her youngest daughter, Daisy, came running onto the terrace, closely followed by Ian. 'My little piglet.' She put an arm around the child. 'And how was Camilla's?'

'We saw *The Wizard of Oz*,' Daisy said.

Diana smiled at her. 'Again?'

Richard gave Daisy a little wave. 'Hi there, Daisy.'

Daisy regarded him coldly and looked straight past him at Lucy.

'You remember Lucy?' said Diana. 'Last time she was here you were only four.'

Daisy examined Lucy with frank, childlike candour. 'What's that?' she said, going over and pointing at Lucy's bracelet.

'It's called a scarab,' said Lucy. 'See? It's like a beetle.'

Ian, who had sat down at the table and was glancing through the newspaper, said: 'There's a political rally in town tomorrow. I was thinking I'd go in.'

'But the shutters, Ian,' Diana protested, 'you promised you'd paint the shutters.'

Ian suddenly looked very tired. 'So I did,' he said.

Daisy transferred her firm stare from Lucy's wrist to her face. 'Want to see something?'

'Sure,' said Lucy.

'Come on, then.'

Diana opened her mouth to speak but Daisy forestalled her. 'You stay there, Mummy.' She grabbed Lucy's hand. 'I'm taking her myself.'

As the two of them went off down the hill, Alex turned to the others and inclined his head. 'I thank you for being so fucking helpful. My God, I can't trust any of you.'

'It was Miranda,' Diana said, 'she wouldn't stop.'

'Me?' Miranda retorted, 'Noemi was, too.'

'What?' said Ian.

Alex, ignoring Ian, said: 'This is an important moment for a girl. You might try to find some sensitivity in your jaded hearts.'

'For what?' Ian said.

Alex continued, as though Ian hadn't spoken. 'She's searching for something, I got the feeling, talking to her last night . . .'

Noemi looked knowing. 'Alex has a crush on her.'

'So that's what it's all about,' Diana said.

'She's after something . . . with those long, slim nervous hands she can barely control and that curiosity and she's a little frightened . . . it reminded me so much of . . .' Alex gazed far into the distance, '. . . myself, somehow.'

Everyone studied the building work on the opposite hill in silence – except for Ian. 'What the hell are you all talking about?' he said.

Lucy followed Daisy through a break in the wall and into a wood. Daisy picked up a couple of plastic

48

bottles and hid them in the foliage. 'Aren't people beastly?'

'Some,' Lucy agreed.

In the distance she could hear the noise of gunshots. She remembered this place. And the stone pagoda housing the peacocks. Niccolo had given her a bright, blue peacock feather; she still had it.

'This is the Donatis',' Daisy whispered. She pointed to the peacocks. 'Wait and they'll put up their tails.' Without changing her expression or her tone of voice she said: 'Mummy said your mother's dead.'

'She is,' said Lucy.

'What happened to her?'

'She took a lot of pills,' Lucy said. She hadn't told anyone that before and she was surprised how easy it was to talk about her mother to this matter of fact child. Nobody else, none of their friends or neighbours, had been so up front about Sarah's death. They'd hedged around the subject: '*So* sorry to hear about your mother, dear . . .' There had been avid curiosity and pity in their eyes. Lucy had hated the pity most of all.

'Why?' continued Daisy.

'She must have wanted to,' Lucy said. 'She tried a few times. She wasn't very happy.'

Daisy nodded understandingly. 'In *The Wizard of Oz* Dorothy's an orphan. She has an Auntie Em. We're only allowed a video recorder with movies. Mummy says that TV breaks up brain cells.'

Lucy laughed. 'Come on,' she said. 'I've been

49

here before.' She led the way down a path until they arrived at the lake and stopped at the stone steps she had looked at so often in her photograph. 'I kissed someone here once.'

Daisy looked at Lucy with interest. 'Did you touch tongues?'

'Uh-huh,' said Lucy. She could hear the sound of banging pots in the far distance.

'Miranda likes to kiss boys,' Daisy confided. 'She always kisses Richard and before that she kissed Matthew and Gianni . . . and Niccolo and David . . .'

'She used to kiss Niccolo?'

'At the fireworks,' Daisy said. 'Hey, what's that?'

Lucy could hear the weird sound of men making yelping noises, the trampling of an animal in flight, a blast of gunfire. 'What . . . ?'

Daisy started to run back towards the peacock pens and Lucy dashed after her. 'Hold it!' She jumped as a gun went off near them, grabbed Daisy's hand, and, as they ran, bent double, glimpsed two lines of men converging in the woods. The boar rushed past them again. Another gun blasted off and Daisy screamed. They reached the peacock pen, and dashed inside. With birds flapping and screeching around her, Lucy managed to fasten the door of the pen. She wasn't sure whether she was more frightened of the birds or the hunters.

There was another rat-tat of gunfire and then, suddenly out of the trees, Alex appeared, supporting himself on his cane. 'Stop shooting!' he cried, in Italian. 'Can't you see there are children here?' The gunfire faded and he called out: 'Are you crazy? You could have killed someone.'

About a dozen men slowly began to emerge through the trees, carrying the pots they had been banging to drive out the boar. One of the hunters stepped forward. 'There has been no danger to anyone,' he said.

'What are you doing here?' said Alex.

'Having a party, what does it look like?' another hunter said.

Lucy led Daisy out of the pen and they came and stood close to Alex.

'Are you all right?' he said.

Lucy gestured with a wobbly hand. 'Just a little . . .'

Alex, furious, turned back to the men, speaking in Italian again. 'Didn't you see these girls here?' He was disturbed to see Daisy shivering as a small boy walked up to her carrying a dead bird. 'This is private land.'

The first hunter took up an aggressive stance. 'We have as much right to be here as they do. It happens to be our country.'

A young man with a mop of curly hair stepped out of the wood. He, too, was carrying a gun. He gestured with it for the others to get back. 'Our country?' he said. 'Too bad we don't know what to do with it.'

The small boy with the dead bird shook it in Daisy's face and she screamed. Lucy was about to put an arm around Daisy's shoulders but the young man who'd been speaking had already loped across to comfort her. 'Stop that, Duccio,' he said to the boy. He fixed the other hunters with a steady gaze. 'Go, please. That's enough for today.'

The men retreated back into the wood, murmuring and muttering. Lucy wondered why this young man had such authority over them and why Daisy looked up at him so trustingly, as though he was an old friend.

'There aren't as many peacocks as before,' Daisy said.

'We've had a *faina*, Daisy.' The young man turned and looked at Lucy. 'You don't remember me.' It was a flat statement, not a question.

Lucy studied him, embarrassed. Should she know him? He was tall and slim. He had brown eyes and a sweet, slightly lop-sided smile. Surely she would have remembered that? 'I don't think . . .'

She was grateful when the young man interrupted quickly, saving her further embarrassment. 'It was four years ago,' he said, in a shy, quiet voice. Leaving Daisy's side, he disappeared back into the wood after the other hunters.

'Come on.' Alex put one hand on Daisy's shoulder and linked the other through Lucy's arm, holding it close to his side. 'Let's go back.'

Lucy was still looking into the wood after the young man. 'Who was that?' she said.

'Osvaldo,' said Daisy. 'He's got a bow and arrow, I've seen them.'

'Niccolo's younger brother?' Lucy remembered a boy – little more than a child – who'd watched her and Niccolo with serious brown eyes. 'I *have* met him,' she said. 'God, he looks so different.'

CHAPTER FOUR

Monsieur Guillaume was sitting at the dinner table, explaining the dishes to Richard, who was examining the food in a way that suggested he'd rather have a large steak. 'This is a *bomba di riso* with delicious pigeon inside, a sort of risotto, I think you'd say, and this . . .' Monsieur Guillaume pointed to another dish, 'is *carciofi ripieni alla mafalda*. Artichokes . . . stuffed.'

'Great,' Richard said unenthusiastically.

'Make some room, someone.' Diana came into the dining room with a pile of plates, followed by Lucy, Daisy and Ian carrying cutlery, salad and a plate of cheeses.

Noemi cleared a space on the table, and handed round the plates. 'And I had been thinking of starting a diet.'

'Miranda, dinner.' Diana looked round for Miranda who waved from the doorway and gestured at the telephone in her hand. 'What?' she shouted down the phone. 'What? No, I'm losing your voice . . . you sound like you're at the bottom of the ocean. You'll have to speak up. I can't hear you. You . . . what? So when will you?' She disappeared from view again and re-appeared to sit down at the table. There was silence as everyone dug enthusiastically into the risotto; except for Richard, who pushed it around his plate suspiciously.

'Who was that on the phone?' Ian said eventually, through a forkful of rice.

'Christopher,' Miranda said.

'Well?' Diana said, after a short pause when it became clear Miranda wasn't going to explain any further.

'They're not coming back.'

Alex, who was looking frail and eating very little, immediately caught Lucy's dejected expression and gave her an encouraging smile, which she ignored. Ever since that awkward breakfast, when everyone had been pairing her off with likely lovers, she'd had difficulty in viewing Alex as a father figure, a trusted confidant, or even a friend.

'Never?' Diana said.

Miranda shrugged. 'I don't know. I couldn't hear properly. They missed a connection or something so it might take another week.'

Monsieur Guillaume wagged his fork at the assembled company. 'Those naughty boys. I bet they're being very, very naughty.'

Miranda raised a cynical eyebrow at Richard and murmured: 'I'm sure they've gone beyond naughty by now.'

Lucy knew that Alex would continue to look at her in that caring, penetrating way and she deliberately kept her eyes on her plate.

'Another week?' said Diana. 'That's typical.' She looked at Ian. 'Isn't it?'

Ian nodded. 'It is. Typical.'

'I don't know why you're surprised if it's so typical,' Miranda said. 'By the way, we saw Carlo Lisca in town.'

'Carlo?' said Diana. 'How's he looking?'

'Lecherous, as usual,' Miranda said.

Lucy looked up at the mention of Carlo Lisca. She'd found letters amongst her mother's belongings from a man called Carlo. They were love letters and they were stamped with the names of indecipherable foreign cities. 'Does he live near here?'

'Near Gaiole,' Diana said, 'when he's not visiting the latest war zone. Why? Do you know him?'

'He was a friend of Mummy's, wasn't he?' Lucy said.

Diana shifted uneasily. 'Yes, he was.' She paused, wondering just how much Lucy knew about Carlo. 'He's a very good war correspondent, but I think seeing so much death, blood and horror has made him a little peculiar.' Gazing brightly round the table, she said: 'Who needs more wine? The Coltibuono is definitely better than ours this year.'

After dinner, Lucy picked up a tea towel and joined Noemi at the kitchen sink. It was a house tradition that, since Diana planned and prepared all the meals, she was excused the clearing up. Noemi, busily scrubbing saucepans, spoke fondly of her own non-stick Tefal pans in Milan and remarked, with great good humour, that when it came to washing up, the Grayson family had an extraordinary ability to disappear from sight. 'Where, for instance, are Miranda and Richard?' she said, passing Lucy a pan to dry. 'And Ian? Gone off to his studio with an artistic glint in his eye, no doubt.'

At that moment Alex limped over, whispered in Noemi's ear, and also left the room.

Monsieur Guillaume joined Noemi and Lucy at the sink. 'Our friend has left us?' He was ineffectually trying to fold the tablecloth.

'Here, let me.' Noemi took the cloth from him and Lucy heard her say quietly: 'He's feeling really awful. He wants to go to bed.'

'Of course,' Monsieur Guillaume regarded her mournfully. 'It should be me, you know.'

Noemi smiled at the old man and gave him the folded cloth to put away in a drawer. 'You must not entertain such thoughts, my friend.' She whirled fresh water around the sink, handed Lucy the final pan, and turned to see Diana grinding coffee beans. 'It's your turn to sit down, darling.' She took the ground beans from Diana and transferred them, swiftly and efficiently, into the espresso machine.

Lucy hung the wet tea towel over the metal bar of the solid fuel stove, vowing to be nicer to Alex next time he gave her one of his meaningful looks. She went over to Diana, who was not sitting down but covering the leftovers in the tureens with clingfilm. 'I'd like to meet Carlo Lisca.'

Diana spent an unnecessarily long time lighting a cigarette. 'Okay,' she said eventually, 'I'll try and get him over.'

'Do you remember Mummy being in love with a man here?'

'You mean Carlo?'

'Well, I don't know,' Lucy said uncertainly. 'There was this thing that she wrote . . .'

'Really?' Diana was intrigued. 'What did she write?'

But before Lucy could answer, Ian appeared in the doorway. 'Lucy,' he said, 'I feel the time has come.'

He strode off towards his studio. 'Off you go, Lucy,' Diana prompted, and watched Lucy follow him out.

Miranda and Richard were entwined on the couch in the sitting room. Richard was kissing Miranda's neck enthusiastically but this did not prevent him eyeing Lucy speculatively as she passed the room with Ian. Miranda was throwing her head back with rapturous delight and he guessed, rightly, that she was unaware of his momentary inattention.

He grinned at Lucy and gave her a wink, but she had her back to him by this time and didn't notice the come-on. He was, however, able to assess the inviting way her body moved under the thin cotton shift thing she was wearing.

Richard considered it fortunate that Miranda was so self-absorbed that she rarely noticed his avidly roving eye. It had certainly fallen appreciatively on Miranda Schermer way back when they'd met at a dinner party in TriBeCa last fall. They'd been sitting around a table on hard little chairs which looked as though they'd been parcelled up in white sheets – Miranda had considered this amazingly chic, for some reason – and he'd immediately been attracted to her rich-girl tan, trim figure and Anglo-American wit. He had just parted from Jeannie after three years of claustrophobic matrimony and was even more susceptible than usual. Jeannie had been a limpet: 'Why were you late home last night, Richard?' . . . 'Where are you going, Richard?' . . . 'Do you still love me, Richard?' In contrast, Miranda had seemed really laid back – boy, had he been wrong about *that* – and he liked the idea of her working for a jewellery designer. It was sophisticated; an impressive, yet feminine thing for a woman to do. They'd had good times together. Miranda was in with the creative crowd and knew all the rich chicks who just had to be seen wearing her boss's expensive jewellery. He'd made a few useful contacts there. Equally, she'd enjoyed rubbing shoulders with his showbiz clients. Rubbing more than shoulders, on several occasions. . . He'd had to prise her away from Jed, lead guitarist and singer in Running Free, the current pop icon and one of his most lucrative clients. The trouble with Miranda was that she liked a bit of rough trade. Richard smiled to himself. To be honest, what Miranda really liked was sex, and that was more than okay with him. He'd wondered how it would be in the bosom of the family, so to speak. But they seemed to be a pretty bohemian bunch and accepted him at face value. Actually, he thought he'd made rather a hit with them; particularly with the mother who was a more than average good-looker in her own right. Might have stood a chance there if things had been different. And what about this new cutie-pie who, so far as he could gather, had come here to zip up her love life? He certainly wouldn't mind lending a hand in that direction.

Miranda raised her head, sensing her lover's distraction. 'Richard?'

'Love ya, babe,' Richard said, and kissed her on the mouth.

Diana and Noemi had gone into the study to phone Carlo Lisca. It was a small, comforting sort of room. The walls, haphazardly washed a pinkish terracotta, were lined with books and there were deep, soft dark green leather chairs in which Diana liked to curl up and read. She was sitting in one of them now, talking to Carlo, in front of a beaten-up pine desk, which Ian had made out of the roof rafters from the old barn.

'But Carlo, we're longing to see you . . .' She grinned conspiratorially at Noemi, who was lounging in the doorway. 'Bring Michele. . . Oh, come on. We've got Lucy Harmon staying. . . yesterday . . . no, alone. Good. Tomorrow then. Tea time. All right. 'Bye.' She put down the phone.

'He's coming?' said Noemi.

'Funny,' said Diana. 'At first he said he couldn't, then when I told him Lucy was here, he changed his mind.' She gazed at Noemi, thoughtfully. 'Ian's gone to the studio . . . You know, he hasn't worked at night for years.'

'Ah,' Noemi said, 'but there's a virgin in the house.'

60

There were times, Diana thought, when she wished Noemi wasn't quite so . . . well . . . *Italian*.

Lucy had never sat for an artist before and she found it very disconcerting. Ian had placed her on a pedestal, studied her from every angle, and then organised her limbs, as though she were an articulated doll, into positions of extraordinary discomfort which he said looked wonderfully natural. She had been trying, unsuccessfully, to stay still while he sketched and ripped off pages, crossly discarding them in a pile on the floor. 'Every time I look at you you're in a different position,' he complained.

Lucy tilted her head on one side and glanced at the nude drawings on the walls. 'It's real cool here.' She looked at Ian. 'My father never came.'

'Some people don't like to leave their country,' Ian said, not looking up. 'You know, I never met your father.'

'He's small,' Lucy said, reflectively. 'I'm five inches taller.'

'Really?' Ian crumpled another page, irritated. 'Maybe if you kept your gaze on that horse's leg, say, it would be easier for you not to move.' He started sketching again on a new sheet of paper and came closer to Lucy, absorbing the sweet softness of her. 'Did you ever notice how in movies the camera is either too far away, or too close?' He came even nearer, still drawing, so his face nearly touched hers. Lucy was bewildered by the intensity of his gaze. 'Now I see where you are different from your mother,' he said. 'You have joy in your eyes.'

Backing away slightly and trying to keep her mouth still and speak at the same time, Lucy said: 'Did you ever eat olive leaves?'

'Olive leaves? They're inedible, disgusting.' Ian's head was bent over his sketch pad and Lucy couldn't see his expression. 'Why do you ask that?'

'Just wondering.' Lucy looked above Ian's head at the skylight. 'I can feel the night over my head.'

'Then you can see why we love it here. One thing I do miss, though. The Gravediggers' – best pub in Dublin.' Ian ripped the page in half. 'I think we've done enough for tonight.'

Lucy stood up and stretched. She felt that she had been a bad model. She kissed Ian lightly on the cheek. 'Sorry . . .'

Ian patted her arm. 'No, you've been very good, very patient.' He watched her leave and slowly put his hand to the place where she had kissed him.

Lucy walked back towards the cottage in the dark. Through an open window she could hear the sound of the wind chimes her mother had muffled. She passed the window and, hearing urgent voices interspersed with heavy breathing and moans, she pressed herself against the wall and listened.

'That feels good. Oh, my God. That's good. I'm your Daddy, baby. Hm . . .'

'Yes, yes, yes . . .' A voice, Miranda's, sobbed the words.

Lucy slipped to the ground. She knew she shouldn't be listening, but couldn't resist it, it sounded so ridiculous.

'No, no, no ... yes, yes, yes.' Miranda's voice rose to a crescendo. Lucy, choking on an involuntary laugh, put a hand to her mouth and knocked over a rake. The sounds inside reached a crescendo and then Lucy heard Miranda say in her ordinary voice: 'What was that?'

Lucy retreated further into the shadows as Miranda and Richard came to the window and looked out. At that moment, Monsieur Guillaume appeared wearing a pair of silk pyjamas. Lucy breathed a sigh of relief as, looking neither to left or right, he walked straight past her and into the pergola.

'What's he doing?' she heard Richard whisper, and Miranda replying: 'Sshh. Don't wake him. You're never supposed to wake sleepwalkers.'

CHAPTER FIVE

She's just a child, Diana said to herself, as she watched Lucy and Daisy screaming and laughing as they raced around the lawn in front of the terrace, playing tag. Lucy was more than twice Daisy's age but in some ways, Diana thought, she seemed younger, more vulnerable. It was almost as though Sarah's death had released her, giving Lucy back her own childhood. Diana's eyes narrowed as Richard joined in the horseplay. He seemed particularly keen on tagging Lucy; perhaps, she decided, a more appropriate name for this game would be 'touch'. She turned to share this thought with Ian but he had been joined by Miranda who was also watching the trio on the lawn, clearly none too pleased to see Richard tumbling an attractive young woman to the ground with such enthusiasm.

Diana's heart ached for her daughter. Miranda always seemed to choose bastards, falling for the designer suit, seemingly incapable of recognising the shoddy quality of the man inside. How many good jobs had she given up for the sake of what she believed to be true love? Diana had lost count, but she could remember Miranda quitting Bonwit Teller, the week after she'd been promoted assistant

64

fashion buyer, to follow a dashing young merchant banker to Singapore; he'd turned out to have a wife in New England. And then she'd taken a course in aromatherapy, and quickly established a client list of Society Names who swore by her essential oils and soothing hands. One had been a druggy film producer – 'Such power, such raw talent, he knows everyone who's anyone in L.A.,' Miranda had assured her mother – who had set her up in a love nest in one of the more expensive cottages in the Beverley Hills Hotel, and then inadvertently killed himself with a toxic cocktail of narcotics. Miranda had been left to deal with three irate ex-wives and the hotel bill. Diana couldn't recall why or for whom Miranda had abandoned her thriving little art jewellery shop in SoHo, but she knew it had something to do with the backer, a Wall Street wizard who'd been heavily into fraudulent junk bonds.

And now this one, with the wandering eyes and hands. Diana sighed, and was relieved to see Carlo Lisca's Saab pull into the drive, causing Richard to relinquish his hold on Lucy, get up and start fussily brushing bits of grass off his clothes.

'It's the Marquis de Saab,' she said to Miranda and Ian. 'He looks even shorter than I remember.'

'Or Michele has grown taller,' Miranda said.

'At twenty-six?' Diana said. 'Hardly. You'll find, my darling, that as you get older there tends to be a certain shrinkage.'

The Liscas wended their way through the terra-cotta figures in the courtyard and eventually

65

reached the terrace to be greeted by Diana, Ian and Miranda. While they were all asking each other how they were and remarking what a long time it had been since they had last seen each other, Noemi appeared with the tea.

'Noemi,' Carlo cried, kissing her. 'What a lovely surprise. You know my son, Michele?'

'Hi.' Noemi bathed Michele in her brilliant smile and wondered how such an extraordinarily ugly man as Carlo could have produced such a handsome son. 'No, we haven't met.'

'Actually, we met once in Rome,' Michele said.

'We did?'

'I remember. I was fifteen.'

Noemi laughed. 'Don't tell me, please, how long ago that was.'

'You were wearing a yellow dress,' Michele said.

'No,' Noemi said. 'I've never had a yellow dress. Not my colour.'

'It had sort of straps,' Michele said, looking at Noemi intently. 'And your back was showing.'

'I'm telling you, I've never . . .' Noemi put a hand on Michele's arm. 'Wait, you know what, actually, I did. I was borrowing it. That was my friend's dress. My God . . .' she looked at Michele in amazement, 'I can't believe you remember that.'

Another conquest for Noemi, Diana thought, pouring out the tea. A rather daunting age gap, of course, but he would do very well for the time being. Noemi always seemed to be passionately involved with one man or another but Diana suspected that the real love of her life had bolted

with Sarah that time. She smiled sadly. Just think
. . . if Sarah hadn't happened by, Noemi might have
been an impoverished Countess instead of one of
the highest paid agony aunts in Italy.

She passed around the cups and saucers and,
leaving Miranda in charge, lit a cigarette and
flopped down on the *chaise longue*. Lucy and Daisy
were now sitting on the lawn engrossed in a book.
She wished Sarah could have been with her to
share the pleasure of seeing their daughters
together. Lucy had Sarah's looks, of course, but she
was much steadier; more like her own Daisy, in a
way. They were both strong, independent charac-
ters. Diana stubbed out her cigarette, closed her
eyes, and turned her mind to what she was going
to give everyone for dinner that evening. There
were times when she grew quite tired of mass
catering.

Ian and Carlo were walking through the trees,
looking at the sculptures. 'You know, Ian,' Carlo
was saying, 'The way I'm feeling at the moment, I
would welcome another war.'

Ian, a pacifist by inclination, was shocked.
'Really, Carlo? I know you're a war correspondent
but . . .'

'Even Sarajevo would be a relief from Marta,'
Carlo said.

'It's that bad, is it?' Ian hoped that Carlo
wouldn't tell him how bad it was; he disliked
intensely being burdened with the intimate details
of other people's lives.

But Carlo had suddenly spotted the girl he'd filmed on the Siena train. 'Who's that?'

'Lucy . . . Lucy Harmon.'

'Sarah's girl?' Carlo said. 'Of course . . .' That's why he'd itched to photograph her, hadn't been able to take his eyes off her; a beauty, just like her mother, but underneath all that perfection . . . Carlo recalled the wanton image of Lucy he'd captured on his video recorder. He wondered if she'd looked at the cassette yet and, if she had, what she'd made of it.

They were now standing in front of Ian's sculpture of a girl sleeping peacefully on the grass. It was Carlo's favourite piece.

Carlo admired it enthusiastically. 'It is perfection. When you come to sell this one, Ian, you'll have to include the grass.'

Ian turned to reply and was surprised to see that Carlo was removing a bracelet – a sort of dark leather looking thing – from his wrist and slipping it surreptitiously into his pocket. He supposed Carlo had a good reason for this odd gesture, but had little interest in finding out what it was.

Ian knew that Diana would accuse him of being insensitive again. 'How can you be an artist without even trying to understand how other people feel and why they behave the way they do?' she was always saying.

Ian usually just shrugged and said nothing which, of course, annoyed Diana even more. The truth was that he believed emotional matters were best left well alone. He had no desire to talk about his own private feelings and didn't see why he should want to delve into anyone else's psyche, either. 'Shall we be getting back?' he said.

The two men returned to the terrace where even Ian couldn't help noticing that Noemi and Michele were engaged in more eye contact than was socially necessary.

'Any girlfriends in Rome?' Noemi was saying. Michele smiled and gave an enigmatic half nod. 'But not the love of your life?' Noemi's eyes sparkled flirtatiously.

Michele blushed, but was still unable to stop himself sneaking a look at the spot where the little silver chain vanished between her breasts. 'No,' he said, finally.

Miranda, hanging on Richard's arm proprietorially, announced that they were thinking of having a swim. This was generally considered to be a good idea, and they drifted from the terrace down the driveway towards the pool. Only Carlo hung back, half waiting for Lucy.

She stepped out from behind one of the terracotta figures. 'Are you Carlo?'

'Yes, I . . .' He hoped she wouldn't recognise him. It would be too boring trying to explain why he had spent so much time squinting through the view-finder at a sleeping girl. 'And you are Lucy.'

Lucy studied Carlo covertly as they moved among the statues, the early evening light casting slanting, shadowy figures on the grass and across their faces. There was a dark menacing quality about him which disturbed her. He reminded her of a toad, squat and somehow slimy; not at all how she'd imagined a war correspondent to be. She'd expected someone tall and lean with the world-weary eyes of someone who'd seen and understood it all. How could her beautiful, glamorous mother have been in love with this ugly little man?

'My mother used to mark a star on her calendar every time she got a letter from you,' she said.

Carlo looked at Lucy sharply. 'How do you know that?'

There was something strangely familiar about his voice. 'I figured it out,' Lucy said. 'She saved all your letters. Did you save hers?'

'I don't save anything,' he said. 'I was very fond of your mother. We had many jokes together. She always appeared to be this elegant woman, but she loved to laugh and act vulgar.'

Lucy tossed her head. 'That's not what I remember. I remember her sitting awake all night in the dark, smoking cigarettes and listening to jazz records.'

'So? Everyone has dark moods.'

'Do you?'

'Only when I'm away from war. Around war I'm as light as a souffle.'

'Have you ever killed a viper?' Lucy asked suddenly.

'Of course,' Carlo said. 'I grew up in the country.'

'In an olive grove?'

'That's where vipers live.' He removed a strand of hair caught in the corner of Lucy's mouth and tucked it behind her ear.

She was touched by this unexpected tenderness. 'Did you ever meet my father?'

'No.'

'He doesn't know about the letters. I spared him.'

'Your mother spared him, too.'

'She lied to him,' Lucy said flatly.

'No, she didn't lie to him. It's not what you think.' Carlo was beginning to be unnerved by this intense child. Why was she forcing him to justify what had been, after all, no more than an amusing interlude? 'We had only one night together,' he said. 'That's all.'

'Only one night?'

'We were friends . . .'

'Lucy!' It was Alex, calling from the studio.

Carlo grabbed at the opportunity to escape Lucy's scrutiny. 'See you later,' he said and strode off briskly towards the swimming pool.

Alex limped out to join Lucy, wishing that he had not found the sight of her and Carlo's shared intimacy so distressing.

'No, no,' he said. 'I don't think he's the one for you. Not for my "Lucy in the Sky".'

'Actually, I rather like him,' said Lucy, wanting it to be true.

'You do?'

'There's something familiar about him.'

'My illusions are shattered.' Alex took her arm. 'Come on. Let us slowly bring up the rear like Turgenev's poor Rakitin.'

They came in sight of the pool and Alex stopped, put a hand over his eyes and groaned. 'Oh, dear.

71

No . . . I can't bear it. Why do they have to do that? Oh God . . .'

'What?' Lucy looked anxiously at Alex and then over at the pool where everyone was gathered, either swimming or lounging on the side. . . They were all glowingly, healthily naked.

'I can't bear it,' Alex said, 'it's too . . . unnatural.' He turned around and began walking slowly back towards the house.

Lucy felt a throb of sympathy and was about to follow him when she heard Carlo and Diana talking. She moved unnoticed towards the voices.

'I felt I was being interviewed,' Carlo was saying.

'She's curious about you,' Diana replied. 'She's really very sweet. But we've been a terrible house of chickens talking about her. You see . . . she's never thoroughly loved someone. Can you imagine Sarah being a virgin at nineteen?'

'It's this generation,' Carlo said. 'They're terrified of disease.'

Lucy turned on her heel and hurried back along the driveway to the house. The conversation made her want to sob with anger and humiliation. It was obvious Niccolo wasn't coming back and she'd had enough of being photographed and stared at, of being the subject of everyone's prurient gossip. She knew that she was not a great one for making decisions. Unlike her mother, who had always seemed so in charge of her life, making exciting things happen, she was the kind of person who sat back and let things happen to her. Well, this time she was going to take control.

*

Back in the cottage, Lucy pulled her duffle bag out from under the bed, threw in her journal without a glance, and piled her clothes on top of it. There was something that felt like a small, hard box inside one of the sweatshirts. It was the cassette from the station. She'd meant to ask Diana if she could borrow the video machine so that she could check it out, and then she'd forgotten all about it. Never mind, she'd look at it when she got home, because that's where she was going and now.

She finished packing and went briskly over to the study. She pulled out the telephone book, looked up Alitalia's number, and was just jotting it down when Daisy appeared in the doorway.

'What are you doing?'

'Looking up a telephone number,' Lucy said.

Daisy came up to her. 'Why?'

'I'm going home, Daisy.' Lucy sat down in the big leather chair and dialled the number '*Si*,' she said, '*A New York. Domani* . . .'

The operator asked her to please hold the line and Daisy climbed on to her lap.

Daisy looked at Lucy pleadingly, 'But what about you having Christopher as your boyfriend?'

'What!' Lucy exclaimed, momentarily forgetting the telephone call. 'What? Where did you get that idea?'

'That's what Mummy told Noemi,' Daisy said.

Lucy rolled her eyes in exasperation. It was definitely time to go. She turned back to the phone. '*Quando? Si*,' she said. '*Scusi . . . scusi . . .*' but the person at the other end had disappeared.

Outside, a car drew up. Daisy, looking through the window behind Lucy, slipped off her lap and rushed to the door to greet a young man with a dusty knapsack.

'Christopher!' Daisy ran into the arms.

'Crazy Daisy.' Christopher picked up his sister and hugged her.

'No! Piglet,' Daisy cried.

'Piglet, then.' Christopher placed a red flag on Daisy's shoulders. 'Hey, here's the Turkish flag.' He looked over Daisy's head at Lucy. 'I remember you . . . Lucy. Did I interrupt . . . ?'

'Oh, no,' said Lucy, hanging up. 'I couldn't get through.'

Somebody else had come into the hall and was calling out in Italian: 'Chris, where do you want this to go?' Lucy recognised the voice immediately.

'Leave it out there, that'll be fine,' Christopher called back.

Niccolo Donati strode into the study wearing an old stained Turkish shirt. Lucy thought he looked even more handsome than the young man in her treasured photograph; leaner, harder somehow, more mature. 'That is the last time I carry your bag,' he said.

Christopher flung an arm around Niccolo's shoulder. 'Look who's here.'

'Daisy . . .' Niccolo said. 'Piglettina.' He looked questioningly at Lucy, standing by the telephone. 'Hullo.'

'*Ciao*, Niccolo,' Daisy cried excitedly, rushing out

74

of the room to spread the news of her prodigal brother's return.

'Don't tell me you've forgotten Lucy,' Christopher said as Niccolo smiled uncertainly. 'Lucy Harmon.'

'Oh, *Lucy*,' Niccolo said. 'I wouldn't have recognised ... but of course it's you.' He turned to Osvaldo, who had followed them in. 'Osvaldo, you remember Lucy?'

'Of course I remember her,' Osvaldo said. 'You coming?'

'Listen, you two,' Christopher said, 'why don't you come back for dinner tonight?'

Niccolo sighed. 'I should see the old lady tonight.'

'Bring her,' said Christopher. 'I'll get Mum to call.'

'Good,' said Niccolo. He looked into Lucy's eyes. 'So, I'll see you very soon.'

Lucy walked back to the cottage with a light step and swiftly unpacked her bag. She went over to the window and watched the Donati pick-up until it disappeared over the hill. The way Niccolo had looked at her when he said he'd see her very soon; it was how she'd imagined it would be, how he'd looked at her that time by the lake. The years of waiting and hoping were over. She could tell, by that look, that he still felt the same way about her as she felt about him. Tonight would be a new beginning for them both. She wondered ... dared to hope ... would Niccolo come back with her to New York? Or, being the elder son, would he want her to stay with him in Italy, to help look after the estate? Lucy breathed in deeply and let out a sigh of pure joy. And then she put on her Walkman and started dancing, wildly, uninhibitedly. She couldn't believe it was possible to feel so happy.

Diana had prepared a supper tray for Alex and was thinking and planning as she carried it over to the cottage. Four more for dinner meant the seafood salad wouldn't stretch. She'd have to raid the *gastronomia* in the village for some prosciutto ... delicious with fresh figs. She'd need to pick some more of those; and a lot more salad stuff. There was an apple tart and masses of cheese in the fridge, but what about the pesto? She must check there was enough for the tagliatelle. She quickened her step.

Alex was lying in bed, raised weakly on one elbow, glimpsing Lucy through the window as she danced madly in and out of his line of vision. Her youth and beauty assaulted his senses and he despised his weakness, hated the gnawing pain eating away at his useless body.

Diana came in with the tray. 'Dinner time.'

Alex fell back against the pillows. 'Do you think she's still angry with me?'

Diana glanced towards Lucy's window. 'Darling, I don't think she's giving you too much thought.' She tried not to see Alex's wistful expression as she shifted the pillows and positioned the tray.

Osvaldo, driving the pick-up, questioned Niccolo about Lucy.

'Yes, we used to write a little,' Niccolo said, 'but I

76

only saw her that one week. And she looked pretty different then . . .'

'I remember she wrote a lot,' Osvaldo said. 'She used to write on top of old postcards.'

'There you go . . . reading my mail again.' Niccolo threw a playful punch at Osvaldo, who was trying to defend himself and drive at the same time. Laughing and wrestling, the two brothers zig-zagged erratically down the hill towards the Villa Donati.

CHAPTER SIX

Chiarella Donati was one of those small, chic women with high cheekbones and a tiny waist who cleverly manage to accentuate their delicate femininity by breeding large, handsome sons. Her arrival, flanked by Niccolo and Osvaldo, was dramatic enough to remind Lucy of her mother. How she would have enjoyed being accessorised with sons, Lucy thought. Once again she had proved herself inadequate.

Chiarella did a cheek-kissing tour of the room, and then took Lucy's outstretched hand in both of hers. 'So, this is Lucy?' She smiled warmly. 'I very much liked your mother . . . except for one small problem. When she was there no man would pay attention to any other woman in the room.' An appealing throaty laugh suggested that this had not, of course, been a problem in her own case, but the laughter wavered slightly as she took in Lucy's slip of a dress, clearly revealing the rounded curves of a young woman.

Lucy smiled back and wished that after all she'd put on one of her droopy black cover-all outfits instead of this one – purely for Niccolo's benefit. She desperately wanted Niccolo's mother to like her, to accept her. Osvaldo had seemed very

78

friendly, but it was Chiarella who really mattered. Lucy was all too aware that Italy was a matriarchal society and that any future with Niccolo would depend to a great extent on Chiarella's approval.

She was trying to formulate a flattering sentence in her mind about Chiarella's beauty being right up there on a par with her mother's when Chiarella suddenly dropped her hand and transferred her attention to her younger son. 'Osvaldo, darling, get your poor old mother a glass of vodka.'

Osvaldo disappeared towards the drinks tray, and Lucy watched Chiarella drift after him, stopping *en route* to greet Noemi and Michele who she'd missed out on her first tour.

Lucy had been too caught up with her own emotions to observe the strength of the bonding going on between Noemi and Michele, but she noticed now that they were standing very close together. Michele was giving Noemi a book in a way that suggested he was handing her something much more valuable – personal. As Lucy went towards them she heard Michele say, 'This is the one I was telling you about.'

Noemi took the book and looked less than pleased when she saw the title. '*Adolphe*, by Benjamin Constant. . . Oh!'

'It's about somebody destroyed by love,' Michele murmured.

'How . . . cheery,' Noemi said. Judging by the bleak way she said it, Lucy presumed that Noemi knew the work and didn't approve of it.

She jumped, startled, as a voice behind her said:

'So, Lucy Harmon. How long are you staying and what do you think of Italy and when are you going to come to our house and see how real Italians live and find out what you've been missing all your life?' She turned quickly to see Niccolo looking at her admiringly, the way his mother had not done.

She returned his gaze reproachfully. 'You didn't even recognise me.'

'You . . .' Niccolo drank from his glass and passed it to Lucy, smiling at her over the rim as he did so. 'You didn't recognise me.' He reached over and helped himself to another glass of wine from Miranda who was passing with a bottle and a handful of glasses. He looked directly into Lucy's eyes, mocking her. 'I know your type, out all night long in those clubs in New York.'

'Not really.' Lucy took a quick, nervous gulp of wine. 'I mean, I've been to some.' She could hear her own voice, silly and girlish, sadly lacking the sophisticated responses she'd rehearsed in her fantasies.

'I picture you perfectly,' Niccolo laughed. 'Dancing your heart out all night.'

'Really,' Lucy said, confused both by his teasing and a heady awareness of his close physical presence, 'I'm really not like that . . . I don't . . . really.' She could feel a familiar warm glow spreading through her body; she knew she was blushing. She longed to get away, to start this conversation all over again at a later date when she'd have all the right answers on the tip of her tongue. She cast around wildly for an escape and, spotting Carlo

Lisca over the other side of the room, ran over to him and kissed him warmly.

Diana, who had been in the kitchen chopping up basil and garlic to augment the pesto sauce, came into the room at that moment and witnessed the affectionate greeting with surprise. 'Dinner's ready,' she said.

They sat under the elms after dinner; Miranda keeping a keen eye on the joint as it passed from Noemi to Michele, to the Donati brothers, and then to Lucy and Christopher. 'And I decided I had to get rid of it in the summer, before I went back to school,' she was saying, as she took the joint and pulled on it deeply.

'Sweetheart, are you speaking of life before me?' Richard wandered down from the terrace to join them. He was staggering slightly as he lay down and put his head in Miranda's lap. He leaped to his feet again within seconds as Miranda lovingly, but inaccurately, struggled to place the joint in his mouth. 'Fuck it, Miranda, now I've got ash all over me.' He shook himself, wiped his face with his handkerchief and made a great fuss of flicking ash off his cashmere sweater. 'That's the pot experience for you.' He sat down again and passed the joint on to Lucy. 'Here we go.'

Miranda ignored his performance. 'So, I ended up doing it with the same guy my best friend did it with. He was the class devirginiser.'

'God, I remember him,' Christopher said. 'He was repulsive.'

81

Miranda nodded agreeably. 'He was creepy, I must admit.'

'I don't remember mine at all,' Christopher said. 'I was completely drunk.' He poured some more wine into Lucy's glass.

She giggled. 'I don't know how we got on to this subject, anyway.'

Noemi looked around her and said: 'What am I doing out here with the children?'

Lucy glanced up towards the terrace where Diana, Chiarella, Ian, Carlo and Monsieur Guillaume were drinking coffee and earnestly discussing politics.

'In this country no one listens to each other,' Carlo was saying, 'everyone stands up with his opinions. It's a country of monologuists.'

Chiarella gave her throaty laugh. 'Are you criticising, Carlo, or using yourself as an example?'

Miranda turned her attention back to the joint which had now circulated as far as Michele. 'And how about you, Michele?'

'I was in a car,' he said. 'It was snowing.'

Miranda looked pointedly at Lucy. 'Lucy?'

The wine and the dope had collided in Lucy's head and she felt totally smashed. 'You're not even mentioning anything to do with falling in love,' she said and was surprised how loud her voice sounded in the still, warm evening air.

'*Il n'y a pas d'amour, il y a que des preuves d'amour,*' Monsieur Guillaume observed sagely, passing them on his way to bed.

Lucy looked questioningly at Niccolo. 'There is

82

not love; there is only proof of love,' he translated. Lucy didn't understand what he meant but she adored the poetic way he said it.

Noemi shrugged, 'Falling in love. That happens much too much. And it's always the first time.'

'No,' Miranda said. 'I've only been in love, I'd say, three-and-a-half times.'

'I was fifteen and by the water,' Lucy said dreamily.

'I was fifteen, too,' Michele said.

Miranda, who seemed to have taken over the role of chairperson, said: 'Who with?'

Michele looked directly at Noemi. 'She was older than me, and wearing a borrowed yellow dress . . .'

'So, what about Osvaldo?' Noemi interrupted swiftly.

'I don't know which is more ridiculous, this conversation or the absurd political one going on over there,' Osvaldo replied firmly.

Lucy rose unsteadily and, weaving around Osvaldo, almost fell against Niccolo. 'You?'

'Not me,' said Niccolo, backing off slightly.

'Not you what?' Lucy said.

'Love is not a word I use.'

Lucy flopped down next to him. 'That . . . that's the saddest thing I've ever heard.'

'I think I miss a lot of mess that way.'

Lucy came closer to Niccolo and whispered in his ear, 'I think I've missed a lot of you.' As she finished speaking her head dropped down between her knees and she threw up into his lap.

'Oh God.' Niccolo jumped to his feet, reluctantly holding her head at arm's length.

Lucy looked up at him, drunkenly unaware of the vomit on her chin. 'No . . . I'm okay . . . Niccolo, what about? . . . you see, he doesn't even remember . . . the steps going down to the lake . . .'

There was a ripple of stoned, barely suppressed laughter. Osvaldo, who wasn't laughing, went over to Lucy and wiped her face with his handkerchief. 'Come on, someone . . .' he looked at Miranda and then at Christopher. 'Christopher. Which is Lucy's room?'

'The cottage,' Christopher said. 'Follow me.'

With Niccolo taking Lucy's shoulders and Osvaldo her legs, they carried her into her room and put her on the bed. She lay there, confused and dishevelled. One of the straps on her dress had snapped and the top was slipping down over her breasts. Osvaldo gently covered her with a sheet. She reached out to embrace Niccolo and Osvaldo signalled to Christopher for the two of them to leave the room.

Niccolo, who was not anxious to be left alone with Lucy, stepped back and attempted to follow them, but she lunged towards him trying to undo his shirt. 'You're too far away . . . too far away . . . for too long.' She was still fumbling with the buttons when she passed out.

Through the partly opened door Osvaldo saw Niccolo wince.

Lucy woke up the following morning wondering

why she felt so ill. There appeared to be a hammer beating rhythmically behind her eyes and her dry mouth tasted disagreeably sour. Doom hung over her in a heavy cloud. She had a vague feeling in the back of her mind that something truly awful had happened last night but she couldn't remember quite what. She felt unable to face herself, let alone the revealing sunlight and collective expressions of distaste from her hosts and her fellow guests. Gloomily she retreated back under the bedclothes.

Diana looked in on her, on her way to take Alex his breakfast tray. 'You all right?'

'Mmmm . . .' Lucy's head emerged tentatively above the sheet. Diana's manner seemed reassuringly friendly and normal. 'I . . . think so.'

'Well, you just stay where you are until you're good and ready to get up.' Diana said. She had cross-questioned Christopher closely over breakfast and knew perfectly well why Lucy felt the way she did. 'Sometimes it takes people days to get over jetlag,' she added kindly.

When Diana had gone, Lucy stumbled out of bed and managed to find a packet of Paracetamol. She washed two of them down with three glasses of water, and went back to bed. She couldn't understand why she still felt so terribly thirsty.

When she woke up again it was early afternoon. She got up, still feeling slightly dizzy, and lay soaking in the hot tub for a long time, thinking.

They were not comfortable thoughts. Why had she gone to bed in her dress, which now lay on the floor in a crumpled heap? She had a gloomy feeling that she had behaved terribly badly and it was something to do with Niccolo. She remembered them talking before dinner, he'd given her his wine. The meal had been delicious and there had been more lovely wine. And then they'd all sat around talking, smoking, drinking . . . and then . . . nothing. Except . . . Niccolo's face. He had looked at her . . . Not the way he'd looked at her at the lake, or when he'd been teasing her about going to nightclubs in New York. The expression on his face had been . . . what . . . disgust?

She towelled herself fiercely, hoping to rub away the troublesome half-memories, and put on her shirt and shorts. She knew she had to see him; to make sure everything was all right between them.

Taking a bike from the shed at the back of the terrace, she wheeled it out and along the driveway. She didn't feel up to riding it.

'Hi!' Miranda caught her up. She was carrying a towel and was on her way to the swimming pool. 'You've surfaced, then?'

'Last night?' Lucy said, pushing the bike and not looking at Miranda. 'Was I all right? I mean, Niccolo . . . ?'

'Fine,' said Miranda. If Lucy didn't remember last night's scene, she certainly wasn't going to enlighten her. 'I know he likes you.'

'Did he say anything?'

'He thinks you're very American.'

'What does that mean?' Lucy looked at Miranda anxiously.

'It's a compliment, I promise. He thinks Americans are great.'

'It doesn't sound like a compliment,' Lucy said doubtfully.

'Lucy, it is.' Miranda turned off towards the pool. 'I'm going for a swim now, see you later. *Ciao*.'

'Right,' Lucy said. She mounted the bike and rode unsteadily towards the Donati villa.

After she'd been pedalling for half a mile or so, she freewheeled down a hill and the gentle breeze in her face, warm, languorously scented with honey, revived her spirits. The tyres of her bike whirred softly in the heavy afternoon silence and the heat reflected from the road enveloped her and made her feel part of the undulating hills and somnolent vineyards in a way she hadn't felt when she'd dashed past in the taxi. She pushed back her hair and quickened her pace; she was eager now to find Niccolo. She smiled and waved at an old woman in a nearby field, pruning vines. The old woman returned a toothless grin and waved back with her secateurs. Lucy breathed in the scented air and slowly expelled it, releasing the tension in her shoulders, the anxiety in her heart. Niccolo would be so surprised to see her, she could picture his smile, the sweet way he'd take her in his arms.

She pedalled slowly down the Donatis' drive and, entering a quiet courtyard, dismounted, leaned her bike against a wall and, stepping through the open front door, called out softly: 'Niccolo?'

There was no reply but Lucy caught sight of a servant mopping the floor in the painted gallery.

She darted out of sight and went swiftly and silently up the stairs, passing a bedroom with an untouched white bedspread, and then a room with a half-unpacked suitcase and a pretty dress hanging in an open wardrobe. In the third room was a pile of folded clothes and, on the top, the Turkish shirt Niccolo had been wearing when he'd arrived at the Graysons.

Lucy went over to the closet, opened it and, for a moment or two, put her face against the white shirts hanging there. And then she wandered around the room, examining a small oil painting, running her fingers over the plaster wall, absorbing Niccolo's aura. On the bedside table was a diary and a pen. Lucy hesitated and then bent down and flipped through the pages. The diary was written in Italian; she recognised the writing and the drawings – inked sketches of places and people. She replaced the diary and carefully pulled out a few strands of her hair and put them under the pillow. On her way out she picked up a book near the door. On the flyleaf was written 'Osvaldo Donati'. She looked at the next book. That, too, was Osvaldo's. Lucy jumped at the sound of an Italian voice in the doorway. 'Are you looking for someone?' It was the same servant she had seen downstairs.

'No,' she said. 'At least, *si*. Is Niccolo around?'

The servant pointed out of the window and replied in Italian: 'He is out there, in the garden.'

Lucy went out of the house and ran down a pathway through the lemon trees. There was a flash of colour by one of the trees. She stopped, stepped back into the shadow of a wall and looked across the lawn. She could just make out a couple standing very close together. The woman was leaning against the tree with her head thrown back and the man was lifting her peacock-blue skirt. Lucy moved slightly away from the wall and concentrated on the back view of the man. It was Niccolo . . .

She fled back to her bike and rode away as quickly as she could, trying, unsuccessfully, to forget what she had just seen. She pedalled fast, faster, half-blinded by tears of misery and rage – anger at herself for obviously having behaved so badly that Niccolo didn't love her any more. Anger at him for betraying her so swiftly and cruelly when she had waited all those years for him. She ignored the small voice at the back of her mind which tentatively suggested that she was taking an awful lot for granted; Niccolo had not, after all, actually *said* he loved her.

She'd hoped to get back to the sanctuary of her room without meeting anyone, but, as she turned a corner in the driveway, there was Osvaldo coming towards her, carrying a dead rabbit. He waved at Lucy energetically. He, at least, seemed pleased to see her. Lucy brushed the tears away with the back of her hand and forced herself to smile and wave back, speeding up her pedalling at the same time so that she wouldn't have to stop and talk to him. She didn't feel capable of talking coherently to anyone. But the bike swerved and went into a dramatic skid, and she fell off, grazing her knee. Naturally Osvaldo rushed up to help her.

'I'm fine,' Lucy said, rising quickly, pretending that her knee didn't hurt.

Osvaldo went to pick up the bike. 'Are you sure?'

Lucy pushed him away. 'Really,' she said, turning to hide the telltale tear stains. She didn't even check on the graze but got straight back on the bike and set off down the drive without a backward glance.

Her mind was in turmoil as she cycled frantically away from the mortifying scene in the lemon grove. What if Niccolo had seen her? What if Osvaldo told his brother that he'd come across Lucy Harmon falling off her bike at the end of their drive? She could feel her cheeks burning with shame, and she was so desperate to get back to the Graysons, that she didn't, at first, notice the car parked at the end of their drive.

'Hullo, there. . . I wonder if you can help?'

Lucy was jolted back to reality. She slowed down, and realised that the voice – Italian, but with a curious accent – had come from a young soldier who was peering helplessly beneath the bonnet of a blue Renault 12. She jumped off her bike and pushed it over towards him. 'Hi,' she said.

He was young and looked really rather charming and old-fashioned in his officer's uniform. He returned her greeting in broken English. 'Hi. It seems I've broken down. I suppose you couldn't . . . I mean, I wonder . . . is there anywhere around here where I can ring for a garage?'

'My friends live at the end of this drive,' Lucy said. 'Why don't you come with me? You can phone from there.'

They walked down the drive together. While the young man spoke earnestly of camshafts and wheel bearings, Lucy was wondering why, when her reason for being was dissolving around her, she'd so eagerly offered assistance. By the time the house came into sight, she decided that it was probably because he was the only man in the neighbourhood who didn't know everything about her; *and* he hadn't been at dinner last night when she'd obviously made such a fool of herself that Niccolo ... her Niccolo ... had ditched her for a girl in a blue dress.

Sarah Harmon always used to swear that Diana was the first person to think of drying flowers and herbs, bunching them together in baskets and dangling them from a wooden clothes-dryer on the kitchen ceiling. 'Such a curious notion,' she'd said to Lucy on their last visit, 'and so clever of darling Diana to have it.'

The Graysons had worked hard to make their house individual and interesting. The patina of the old woods Ian used for the furniture glowed from the attentions of his craftsman's caring hands, and Diana instinctively and economically created the sort of harmonious decor that gets featured in Sunday supplements. They'd also had no hesitation in enlisting the help of their friends. Sarah had been encouraged to donate her antique Paisley shawl to the battered green velvet sofa ('It looks so much better on it than on me, darlings . . .') and, when Diana and Ian were converting the barn, even Monsieur Guillaume had been despatched to the Town Hall in Siena, to look through the archives and check that the architrave around the doorway was authentically in period.

This afternoon, Noemi, who had painted much of the Graysons' property and belongings over the years, was crouched in the shade of the elms helping Diana renovate a couple of old kitchen chairs. Noemi had finished painting the dark, spruce green base, and Diana was cutting a stencil for the backs of the chairs when she saw Lucy coming up the drive accompanied by a man in uniform.

'It looks as though Lucy has a policeman in tow,' she said.

'He doesn't look like a policeman to me,' said Miranda, from the depths of a deckchair where she was stringing beads.

Noemi glanced up eagerly. She adored meeting new men.

Lucy was aware of a flutter of feminine interest as she brought the soldier over and explained his dilemma.

'You know where the phone is in the study, Lucy,' Diana said. 'You'll find the number of the local garage in a clip on the desk.'

'So?' Diana enquired, when they had phoned and returned to the garden. 'Can they fix it?'

'The garage are sending for a spare part,' the

young man said. 'They promised it for early tomorrow morning.' He bowed to Diana and then to Lucy and turned to go. 'Thank you, anyway.'

Lucy put out a restraining hand. 'But . . .'

'No, stay,' Miranda said.

Diana smiled at him. 'You can't just go and sit at the bottom of the drive. Of course you must stay here.'

Miranda went over to the tea table. 'Would you like some tea?'

'Well . . . thank you.' The young man sat down, overwhelmed by the unexpected attention and hospitality.

Miranda handed him a cup and saucer. 'Are you in the Highway Patrol?'

'Thank you,' he said, taking the tea. 'No, the army. French.'

'You're French?' Diana said, in the surprised tones of someone who might never have heard of the French having soldiers. 'You must have some of our honey – from our own bees.' She offered a plate with a slice of bread dripping with butter and honey. 'Do you have a . . . what is your rank?'

'Lieutenant.' The young man took the plate and balanced it uneasily on his knees. 'Thank you.'

'Your English is very good, Lieutenant,' Noemi said.

Monsieur Guillaume appeared on the terrace and seemed delighted to come across a fellow countryman. '*Bon soir. Comment ça va?*'

'*Bien, merci*,' the Lieutenant said.

Diana dumped the paint brushes into a jar and

smiled hopefully at her assorted guests. 'I know. Why don't we all go down to the Pizzeria for dinner tonight? And you'll join us, I hope, Lieutenant?'

'Well, *merci*,' he said.

'Where did you find him?' Miranda hissed at Lucy at the same moment as Diana noticed Lucy's grazed knee.

'Lucy, darling, what have you done to yourself?'

Lucy didn't answer Diana's question. 'At the bottom of the drive,' she said to Miranda.

Although falling off a bike was not in the same league of embarrassment as having your sex life – or, even more dire, the lack of it – dissected and discussed by everyone around you, Lucy thought it was still a pretty stupid thing to do and she was keeping quiet about it. But her knee was beginning to throb and could no longer be ignored. She left the others on the terrace and went off to her room in search of ointment.

Alex was asleep outside the cottage, hooked up to the IV and Lucy noticed, as she came out with her tube of antiseptic ointment, that his book had fallen off his lap. She picked it up and although she replaced it very gently, so as not to wake him, his eyes instantly blinked open; a direct gaze that surprised her.

'Don't be angry with me any more,' he said. 'I am sorry. Really.'

Lucy saw that he was weaker and that his limbs seemed even more awry and unmanageable today than they had been yesterday. It was impossible to go on being cross with him and, sitting down on the ground next to his chair she squeezed out a fingerful of ointment and, as she rubbed it on her knee, said: 'We're all going to a Pizzeria for dinner tonight – if you want to come.'

Alex managed a thin smile. 'I think I'll pass on that.' He put out a hand and squeezed her shoulder, a gesture of thanks. 'What have you done to yourself?'

'It's just a scratch. It's okay.'

'Hold on a minute.' Alex fumbled with the IV, unhooked it, with difficulty, from the centre of his chest and breathed a sigh of relief at being free of tubes. 'Now, come with me, I've got some stuff for that knee.'

Lucy followed him into his room and sat on the bed. Alex limped over to a chest, fetched a bottle of alcohol and a bandage and came and sat next to her.

'You know, Lucy, you mustn't let it get to you.'

'What?'

'Us. We don't mean any harm. It's just that up here, on this hill, we've got nothing much to talk about except each other.' He poured some alcohol on the scratch.

'Ouch!' Lucy cried. 'Would you blow, please?'

Alex blew on her knees. 'Please forgive me.'

'I'm not mad any more,' she said truthfully. 'Just feeling ghastly from last night.'

'I hope you mean it. I feel as if you've given me a sort of injection, much better than an IV. A living injection.' He wound a bandage around her knee. 'Do you know French?'

95

She nodded. '*Comme çi, comme ça.*'

'*L'immense frivolité des mourants* . . .' He tied the knot on the bandage. 'So . . . you must indulge my immense frivolity.'

'Thanks.' Lucy got up and kissed him. 'It's okay,' she said, 'really.'

She went into her room and had just finished washing and changing into a yellow linen shirt when Alex called out: 'So, how's it going?'

'How's what going?' Lucy came out, brushing her hair.

Alex was leaning against the doorway. 'The mission. Don't be discouraged.'

'It's not a mission,' she said and went straight back into her room so that he wouldn't see her irritation. What was the point of Alex apologising if he just went right on prying and questioning? Anyway, she wasn't absolutely sure that yellow was the ideal colour to complement her hung-over complexion.

Alex noticed, as Lucy reappeared, that she had changed out of the yellow shirt into something drably grey. 'The other shirt was better . . .'

Lucy, wearing the recommended yellow shirt, led the way into the Pizzeria, followed by the Lieutenant, Noemi and Michele.

'Alas,' the *cameriere* spread his hands in regret. 'As you see, we are totally full . . . another half hour, maybe?' Then his professional eye lit upon Diana and Ian bringing up the rear of the party. '*Signori!* I did not realise it was you.' In a matter of minutes he had summoned up four tables, put them together, covered them with a cloth and sat the party down.

Two carafes of Chianti appeared and everyone ordered aperitifs. Lucy had a prudent fresh orange juice.

Ian, sipping a Martini and soda, spoke to the Lieutenant in Italian. 'And what brings you to these parts, Lieutenant?'

'Please,' he said, 'I like to practise my English. I'm here for work. Unfortunately, not something I am permitted to discuss.'

'Top secret, eh?' Richard was impressed.

'Top secret . . .' Noemi's eyes sparkled mischievously at the young soldier.

'Mission thwarted by a stalled car,' Michele

murmured in her ear. He'd noticed the sparkle and didn't care for it.

'Why, look who's here,' said Christopher. They all turned and followed his gaze. Osvaldo, Niccolo and a girl in a peacock-blue dress were coming through the door. 'Come and join us.'

Lucy, sitting next to Daisy, busied herself unbuttoning the child's cardigan, as the Donati brothers and the girl came over to their table. The girl had a rather hard face, Lucy thought.

'Thank you, but no,' Niccolo said. 'You've already started. We'll just . . . this is Gabriella.'

'Oh, Gabriella,' Christopher said, unenthusiastically.

The rest of the party nodded politely and Niccolo shepherded the girl towards another table. Osvaldo paused and put a hand on Lucy's shoulder. 'Did you hurt yourself?'

'Why?' Miranda said. 'What do you mean?'

Lucy, arranging Daisy's cardigan on the back of her chair, didn't answer.

'She fell,' Osvaldo said, and went off to join Niccolo and Gabriella.

'Can I see where?' Daisy turned to Lucy, full of interest.

'Not just now—' Lucy began, but was interrupted by Monsieur Guillaume at the head of the table, who suddenly shouted: 'Never in my life . . .'

They all looked up in surprise and Diana was disturbed by the hint of vacuousness in her friend's face. 'Does anyone want more bruschetta,' she said, diverting the moment. 'Lieutenant?'

'Thank you, no.'

'Get this shit off the table,' Monsieur Guillaume cried.

Everyone concentrated purposefully on their food, except for Lucy who was covertly watching Niccolo.

Eventually, Christopher said: 'Are the angels talking again, Mister G?'

'I can't piss in that shitpile.'

'Uh-oh,' Diana sighed. She'd realised, of course, when Guy had arrived for his annual visit a month ago that he was just that bit more forgetful than he had been last year, that his mind was slipping away, disintegrating, but she'd been too busy worrying about Alex to do more than mention it to Ian, who had said he didn't know what she was fussing about, Mister G seemed perfectly all right to him.

'Have I said something wrong?' the Lieutenant asked her anxiously.

'He's a very well-known art historian, a genius really, but he has these episodes,' Diana said, almost under her breath.

'What is it, Guy?' Ian's tone was hearty; he was all too aware that the rest of the room was hushed, alert with interest.

Monsieur Guillaume's voice rang out in the silence. 'When you visit, please fuck your mother.'

Diana rose and looked around the table. 'He was out in the sun, he's exhausted.' She went up behind the old man and gently put her hands on his shoulders. 'Guy, how about we take you home? *Tu es fatigué.*' She took one of his arms and Ian took the other.

'*Tu es une jolie slut,*' Monsieur Guillaume called out, without moving. 'Come, suck the shoes of history.'

'Monsieur Guillaume is very theatrical,' Daisy said, nodding sagely at Lucy who, with her attention divided between Niccolo in the far corner and Monsieur Guillaume at the head of the table, was beginning to feel that they were all taking part in one of Ibsen's more obscure dramas.

The Lieutenant rose. 'Perhaps I could . . . ?'

'I think we can manage, thank you,' Ian said.

Catching sight of the Lieutenant, Monsieur Guillaume lowered his voice and, speaking in French, said: 'My friend, I'm sorry I haven't a car for you.'

'That's quite all right,' the Lieutenant replied, also in French. He came over to the old man. 'You see, I prefer walking. Would you care to join me?'

He offered Monsieur Guillaume his arm. Much to everyone's surprise he rose and took it. 'That's most kind of you.'

They went out of the Pizzeria together, followed by Diana and Ian. The Lieutenant returned in a few minutes and sat down at the table. 'The old man is not well.' He shook his head sadly. 'Mr and Mrs Grayson have taken him home in the car. They said to tell you that they will see you all later.'

'You handled the situation beautifully,' Noemi said. 'Such *delicatesse.*'

'Mmm,' Michele murmured.

They finished their pasta and pizzas quickly,

hardly speaking. Lucy took a further quick glance at Niccolo's table and got up. 'I think I'll walk home.'

'Hold on,' said Richard, reaching for his wallet. 'We're almost done.' He put the money and the bill down on a plate and handed it to the *cameriere*.

'No, I'd like to walk,' Lucy said. 'It's not that far.'

'Is it safe?' said Richard.

'Of course it's safe,' Miranda said. 'You're not in Manhattan now.'

The Lieutenant smiled at Lucy. 'I'll come with you, if I may. I like to walk myself.'

Lucy and the Lieutenant strolled in silence along the road. The sky was full of stars, crickets hummed in the hedgerows and there was a scent of wild lavender and honey in the night air. A few cars went by and then one of them stopped. The Lieutenant flashed his torch, lighting up Richard in the driver's seat.

'Sure you don't want a ride?'

Lucy glanced at the Lieutenant. 'We're sure.'

As they drove off, Richard said: 'You think she's safe with him?'

'When did safety suddenly become such a concern?' said Miranda.

'A military man,' Noemi remarked from the back seat. 'Definitely better for Lucy than Niccolo.'

Miranda was becoming more and more aware of Richard's interest in Lucy and was getting rather tired of her being the centre of attention. 'Haven't we gotten tired of talking about Lucy yet?' she said.

Richard scowled at her. 'I thought you were the

one who was so fascinated by the house virgin.' He put his foot down hard on the accelerator pedal causing Miranda and Noemi to lurch forward in their seats. The rest of the journey passed in silence.

When they had been walking for about ten minutes Lucy put a hand on the Lieutenant's arm. 'Listen.'

They could heard singing in the distance. Without a word they followed the voices – down a lane, through a dark cloister and into a refectory. The scene reminded Lucy of a Christmas card; mellow candlelight glowed on the wood panelled walls, illuminating a group of monks robed in white, and a picture she recognised as Ghirlandaio's 'Last Supper'. It took her breath away. There was a depth of colour in the painting which had been lost in the print she'd studied in her History of Art class. The monks didn't look up as the two of them slipped into the back of the hall, but continued singing in perfect harmony.

'They're Dominicans . . .' the Lieutenant whispered. 'A Gregorian chant.'

They stood quietly for a moment, and then the Lieutenant joined in the singing. He had a pure voice and perfect pitch. Lucy closed her eyes, completely relaxed, as the cadences of the chant echoed through the old building.

The singing stopped and she heard the Lieutenant say: 'Oh, I am so sorry . . .'

She opened her eyes as one of the monks came up to them and said courteously: 'Excuse me, we are recording here.'

A sound recordist emerged from behind a podium and looked at them in surprise.

'Forgive us, please.' The Lieutenant bowed to the monks and the sound recordist. He took Lucy's hand and they walked quickly out of the refectory and back onto the road.

'That was beautiful,' Lucy said.

'The night is beautiful,' said the Lieutenant. They walked along, hand in hand, until they arrived at his car. 'And now I must thank you for being my chaplain.'

'You mean chaperone,' said Lucy. 'You could stay at the Graysons, you know.'

'I'm okay here.' The Lieutenant opened the driver's door, lighting up the car. 'Besides, I want to get up early.'

On the dashboard Lucy could just make out a snapshot of a young woman and two little girls. 'Is that your family?' She got into the driver's seat to look more closely at the photo. 'You have two girls? What's your wife's name?'

'Annunziata,' the Lieutenant said.

'Sounds holy . . .' Lucy slid over to the passenger seat and the Lieutenant looked around apprehensively and then got in next to her. 'What's your name?'

'Leonardo.'

'The names here are so kind of . . . major,' Lucy said. She turned on the radio. An old American song was playing . . . 'It had to be you . . . it had to be you . . . I wandered around and finally found somebody who . . .'

They looked into each other's eyes. Leonardo dropped his gaze first and reached across to open Lucy's door. 'You are a pretty girl and very young and I am going to sleep.'

Lucy leaned against his outstretched arm and, moving closer, put her arm around his neck. Leonardo hesitated for a moment, and then bent to kiss her. Still kissing her, he gently placed her hand on his crotch, rubbing it up and down. Lucy started nervously, her eyes flew open. His mouth was on hers and he was rubbing her hand harder and harder. And then, to her astonishment, he threw back his head and swore in French. Lucy went on rubbing half-heartedly, not sure quite what was expected of her.

Suddenly, Leonardo pushed her hand away. '*Vai, vai,*' he shouted. 'Get off.'

'What?' Lucy was perplexed. 'What? Did I . . . ?'

Leonardo, who had begun to find the situation frustrating as well as embarrassing had spoken more angrily than he'd intended. 'Listen, not attracted enough. Can't you tell? Go on. Get out.'

Lucy slowly opened the door, and glanced back at him.

'Go on.' He pushed her.

Lucy stumbled and half fell out of the car. She walked quickly away up the drive. In the distance she heard the car door slam.

The house was silent as she crept into her room and quickly undressed. She got into bed and pulled the covers over her head. God, how she hated being young and stupid and . . . and . . . innocent. What a fool she'd just made of herself. She thought of Miranda and the class devirginiser. It was the same story with most of the girls in her year at college. They all appeared to lose their virginity with such panache, swapped rings and pins and whispered confidences and then either settled into coupledom or moved on to the next guy. And she had remained aloof, saying, 'No, sorry, I can't make it tonight . . . no, please, I'd rather not . . . yes, there is someone else . . .' She'd invested her desires in memories of a handsome young man by an Italian lake, and the words of a letter she'd carried in her heart for four years. Well, a flash of blue silk in the lemon grove had finished that fantasy. How she'd deluded herself. She turned over and gazed sightlessly at the ceiling. What was the matter with her, anyway?

Early next morning there was nothing but a pile of cigarette butts on the ground where the Lieutenant's car had been. Lucy looked at them, unsettled. Why were relationships so uncool? Did everyone go through these same nightmare situations, or was she uniquely unlucky? You're only young once, people were always telling her, rather tiresomely. Make the most of it while you can. Well, she'd tried and all she seemed to get in return was rejection and flesh-crawling embarrassment.

Monsieur Guillaume stood in a nearby vineyard, waving fondly as a car was slowly towed away across the valley. Lucy watched the car disappear over the brow of the hill, only slightly comforted by the thought that it was taking the young soldier with it. And, thank God, nobody else had witnessed her humiliation.

She tried, none too successfully, to regain her composure as a car drew up beside her and Michele called out: 'Hi, Lucy. What are you doing up so early?'

'Oh . . . hi.'

Michele, who was a kindly young man, could see that Lucy was upset about something. 'I'm just going into Siena,' he said. 'Do you want to come and have breakfast with me?'

'Why not?'

They found a small cafe just off the via di Citta and Michele ordered cappuccinos and toasted ham and cheese sandwiches. Lucy refused the sandwich, she knew it would stick in her throat, but accepted a cigarette. She seemed to have been smoking an awful lot recently.

'Did you know that my mother slept with your father?' she said.

Michele leaned over and lit Lucy's cigarette. He didn't seem surprised. 'I couldn't begin to count all the women my father's slept with. He's one of those men who has to jump on every woman he sees. He can't help it. I'm surprised he hasn't tried it with you.'

'I think her first affair was with her shrink,' Lucy said.

'Women always fall in love with their shrinks,' Michele said. 'My father should have gone into that profession.'

'He told me he only slept with my mother once.'

'What?' Michele said incredulously. 'I'm sorry. My father may be a journalist but he is not famous for telling the truth about his life.'

Lucy studied Michele curiously. 'Oh,' she said. 'I wonder . . . ?'

Michele did not want to talk about Lucy's mother or his father; he wanted to talk about himself. 'Enough of parents,' he said. 'We'll take a walk.'

He paid the bill and they wandered down the narrow street, passing small, expensive shops and old stuccoed houses, streaked in the palest shades of ochre and terracotta, and into the heart-shaped Piazza del Campo. It was made golden by the sunshine, already slightly dusty and bustling with students meeting and greeting at pavement cafés, and thick with tourists sitting by the Fountain of Joy, photographing the marble palaces and each other and watching the rest of the world hurry by.

'This is where they hold the horse race, twice a year,' Michele said. 'Come.' He led Lucy through a pretty inner courtyard and into the Palazzo Pubblico. 'Now, we climb the bell tower and have one of the best views in all Tuscany.'

Beyond the green and white marble tower of the cathedral, the clustering roofs of Gothic and Romanesque buildings and the mellow walls of the Medici fortress, Lucy could see vineyards reaching out to the horizon. It was a calming, peaceful sight. 'I'm glad we came here,' she said. 'Thank you.'

'It's a good place for a troubled mind,' Michele said.

'You're troubled?' Lucy was disconcerted. She'd thought she was the only one with troubles; Michele had always seemed so carefree.

'I'm not like my father, you see.' Michele was looking out over the panorama of the city and not at Lucy. 'I'm much more shy with women. I can't even tell if a girl is interested. They always seem to act not interested.'

'Girls don't usually show when they're interested,' Lucy said wisely. 'It's not considered cool.'

'So, how do you tell?'

'You just have to try.'

'Even if she ignores you?'

'Well . . .' Lucy hesitated. 'Yeah.'

Michele moved closer and said confidentially, 'But it's so hard to go about it. What if she laughs at you?'

So, Lucy thought, maybe I'm not the only innocent in this world. 'I doubt she would.'

'Really?' Michele seemed relieved. 'So you think, just be bold . . . ?'

Lucy smiled at him encouragingly. 'Definitely.'

'Do you know who I'm talking about?' Michele looked at her directly. 'I think you do.'

Lucy pretended to consider the matter.

'Do you think she's interested?'

'I think she might be,' Lucy said, liking him. 'I bet she is.'

'You don't think the age difference is too great?'

Surprised, Lucy said: 'How old are you?'

'Twenty-six.'

'Not at all.'

'The thing is,' Michele said, 'I've always liked older women. They have more . . .'

Lucy, taken aback, said hesitantly: 'Exactly, how old is she . . . exactly?'

'Noemi?' Michele smiled tenderly. 'I think, maybe forty-five. She's so . . . exciting.' He gave a nervous self-deprecating laugh. 'It's silly, I know, but I have her face stuck in my brain. Has that ever happened to you?'

Lucy gazed across the vista towards the Castello di Brolio and the Villa Donati which she knew was close by. 'Yes,' she said. 'It's happened to me.'

'Noemi kind of lights up when you come on the scene,' Lucy told Michele, on their drive back from Siena. She'd got over her initial discomfiture at finding out that Michele had been talking about Noemi, not her, and rather liked the idea of influencing somebody else's romance. It certainly made a change from being the sole object of everyone else's vicarious interest.

'But, she's an Italian,' Michele had said, as though that explained everything.

'True,' Lucy had agreed. 'Even so, for you it's mega-watts.'

Michele had left her, reassured. 'You have given me courage, Lucy. I will be bold.'

When they got back, Lucy returned to her room and washed her hair. She always found the sensation of water pouring over her head remarkably therapeutic. Putting on the large, comfortable shirt she'd filched from her father's wardrobe before she left New York, she took out her journal and, going over to the window sill, looked out across the vineyard. She lit a cigarette and wrote: 'I wait, I wait so patiently . . . I'm quiet as a cup . . . I hope you'll come and rattle me. . . Quick, come wake me up.'

It was how she felt, it sort of said what she meant it to say, but wasn't the simile a bit odd? She couldn't imagine Emily Dickinson or Virginia Woolf comparing themselves to cups. She left the scrap of paper on the sill, put her journal aside, and began drying her hair.

There was a knock at the door. 'Who is it?' she called out. Nobody replied, so, still towelling her hair, Lucy went over and opened it. Outside Richard was bending and stretching and flexing, breathing deeply in time with his exercises: 'Ooh, ah, ooh, hmm, hmm, ooh . . .' He was dressed for jogging and wearing sunglasses. Lucy thought he looked pretty stupid.

'Hi.' He stood still and looked at her uncertainly for a moment, as though he couldn't quite remember why he was there. 'I was wondering . . .' he said, spotting Lucy's cigarette, 'if maybe I could bum a smoke.'

'I thought you hated smoking,' she said, not budging from the doorway.

'Don't tell Miranda. I really have to quit, someday.' He pushed past her and came into the room. 'So, I've never been over here before.' He gazed around, impressed. 'Wow, it's like a loft, isn't it? I had one in SoHo, but the bathroom wasn't completely exposed to the whole room.' He picked up her journal. 'And what have we here? So, you do write, eh? What do you write ... your fantasies?' Lucy took the journal from him and handed him a cigarette.

She sat on the bed at the other side of the room, which was as far from Richard as she could get.

'You remind me of a cat,' he said.

'I don't really like cats.'

'A little cat. You do have fantasies, don't you?'

'Everyone does.'

'Things you would ever act on?' Richard had taken off his sunglasses and Lucy was disquieted by the look in his eye. She gave a non-committal shrug.

'There's an exercise actors do to shed their inhibitions. Have you ever tried that? Giving up control?'

'How?' She was watching him with suspicion.

'You do what the teacher says.'

'I'll bet.'

'No,' Richard said, 'it's not like that.'

'Like what?' she said, confused.

'Like, get on your knees.'

'On my knees?' Lucy couldn't believe she was having this conversation. 'You're kidding ...'

'I'm going to show you.' He smiled at her encouragingly, as though she was a particularly recalcitrant pupil.

Lucy stubbed out her cigarette and considered

111

the invitation. 'Okay,' she said eventually, 'if you do it first.'

'Right,' Richard said, kneeling down. 'First . . .' She came over and knelt beside him, noticing, as she did so, that he was wearing rather a lot of aftershave. 'Now on all fours.'

Lucy suppressed a nervous giggle. 'Oh, really . . . I don't think this is very—'

'No talking,' Richard said. They both went down on all fours, and he turned to her. 'Now, go to the mirror, slowly.'

The two of them crawled across the room and faced the floor-length mirror. 'Okay,' he said. 'Open your mouth.' Lucy opened her mouth. 'Tongue out.' She put out her tongue. 'Lick.' She looked at Richard, who was licking the mirror. Was he crazy or something? She licked the mirror. 'Like a cat . . .' He licked the mirror again. 'Good little kitty. Miaow . . . and lick. One more time.' His tongue was just beginning to stray towards her tongue when, mercifully, there was someone at the door.

'Lucy, have you seen . . . Richard? Oh!' It was Miranda. Richard scrambled to his feet and Lucy flopped back against the wall.

'What the hell's going on in here?' Miranda shouted and slammed out of the room.

Richard followed her. 'Sweetie, you know, we were just . . . wait a second . . . wait . . .'

Lucy, collapsing on the bed, heard them pass her window.

'Frankly,' Miranda was saying, 'I don't know why you came. Either you're jogging your ass off, or you've got your ear glued to the phone. Plus, you reek of aftershave. What were you two doing in there, anyway?'

'Nothing,' Richard said.

'For Christ's sake. You were in there sniffing around her like a dog.'

'Miranda . . .' Richard's voice was cringingly conciliatory. 'She was asking me about . . . Lee Strasberg's acting techniques.'

'No, no.' Miranda snorted in disbelief. 'I'm sorry, no. Don't ask me to believe that.'

Lucy lay back and put her hands over her face. God, she thought, another disaster. I've done it again. How could I have got myself into this one? Am I a masochist, or what?

She got up, went over to the basin and washed her red face. Her hair, reflected in the mirror, was wildly awry. She brushed it fiercely, and wondered, with mounting panic, how she was going to face Miranda over lunch.

CHAPTER EIGHT

It was that calm, aimless time of day when everyone lounges about on the terrace drinking long, cool spritzers and deciding what to have for lunch.

'Just a simple pasta, maybe?' Richard said, causing Diana to regard him with considerable dislike. It was her opinion that there was no such thing as a simple pasta just as there was no such thing as a simple salad. Both involved a good deal of fiddling with knife and grater and she had no intention of doing either. Besides, she'd invited the Donati boys over for a drink, and she didn't know yet when they were coming or whether they might stay for lunch.

'I thought a picnic?' she said tentatively.

Noemi, sorting piles of herbs, responded immediately and loyally: 'A plate of bresaola drenched in olive oil, some delicious provolone and a loaf of bread. What could be nicer and what could be easier to prepare? I will do it.'

Richard, who didn't like his meat cut thin, glowered ungraciously. He poured himself a drink and dialled a German number: '*Nein, nein, hor doch zu, ich weiss was wir machen mussen . . .*'

Miranda, sitting apart on a rock in the middle of the lawn, regarded Richard resentfully. She hadn't been taken in for a moment by that let-me-teach-you-Lee-Strasberg's-acting-technique boloney. Richard had been trying to get his leg over, no doubt about it, and she was sorely tempted to get rid of him there and then, trade him in for another model. Frank, the jewellery designer, sprang to mind. True, he was an asshole, but he was a rich asshole with a lot of charm and talent and he'd made it clear to his favourite pupil, on more than one occasion, that he was available if she was interested. And he'd be prepared to back her if she wanted to start up her own business. Miranda thought about Frank who was five foot eight and marginally overweight and looked again at Richard, this time more favourably. Maybe she'd give him another chance. He was fun and he was fit, a uniquely agile lover. Anyway, he wasn't entirely to blame. Ever since Lucy Harmon had turned up there had been an almost claustrophobic miasma of sensuality drifting over the Villa Grayson. It reminded Miranda of the kennels where she'd lodged Herman, her German Shepherd puppy, when she and the shit bond trader had gone down to Fire Island for a long weekend. They'd had a bitch on heat in one of the compounds and all the dogs were restlessly yelping and drooling, their tongues lolling in hopeful anticipation. . . Not a million miles away from the current scene chez Mummy and Step-Daddy, with every red-blooded male lusting after Miss Youth and Innocence. Miranda was convinced she'd even detected a half-forgotten gleam in the eye of poor old Guy Guillaume. Christopher, at least, was immune to Lucy's lush promise.

God, how she'd worried about him in New York when the AIDS thing started, but he seemed okay. He'd turned up at one of Frank's parties with a steady sort of guy, a set designer who'd told her more than she'd wished to know about the great cooking utensils he'd bought in Zabar's that morning. She'd never talked to Christopher about his sexual preference because he'd deliberately side-stepped her leading questions, and she hadn't liked to discuss it with her mother since she still seemed to be clinging to the illusion of distant wedding bells. Miranda had even heard her suggesting that Lucy and Christopher might be an item. For a while she'd entertained an idle thought or two about Niccolo, what with the two of them traipsing around Turkey together, but you only had to see the way he looked at Lucy – or any other female, for that matter – to know that he and Christopher had been bonding in purely old pals mode.

It was obvious that Michele's interest was focused elsewhere. Miranda loved Noemi. She'd known her since she was a child, had seen unsatisfactory lovers come and go, and longed for Noemi to be happy. So what if she was almost old enough to be his mother. She didn't look like his mother, for God's sake, and age was irrelevant these days. You could always have that in-vitro whatsit, like that Italian woman who'd produced at fifty-five. Miranda considered Michele – his slim hips and dark

116

brown eyes, his adorable nature and his column in *La Stampa* – fast becoming a must-read amongst the informed political groupies – and decided he was a perfect match for Noemi. Luckily, he showed no sign of taking after that nasty hedonistic father of his. Carlo ... there was another one apparently drooling over Lucy. And Alex, darling Alex, at death's door but watching her every move with hungry eyes, consumed by a hopeless passion. Miranda, temporarily and uncharacteristically forgetting herself, was engulfed by sadness.

She glanced over at Ian, who was under the elms, sketching Lucy, absorbed in his work. Even Ian, dear, stalwart Ian who, Miranda knew, loved her mother devotedly, seemed to be more concerned with his sitter than was strictly, artistically necessary ...

Lucy sensed Miranda looking at her but knew she mustn't move and turn around to check on her expression. She just hoped Miranda didn't imagine that she had been planning to entice Richard away from her with that bizarre cat routine. It was Lucy's view that Richard Reed was the boyfriend from hell; she couldn't imagine what Miranda saw in him.

She'd been sitting there for half an hour now and was just deciding whether or not she was getting muscle cramp in her left leg, when Daisy sprang out from behind the tree.

'Hi, Lucy. Want to play?'

'Sorry . . .' Lucy smiled and surreptitiously shifted her leg.

'Oh, come *on*,' Daisy said. 'What's the matter with you, anyway?'

'Daisy, Lucy's helping Daddy with his work,' Ian said patiently. 'Go and find someone else to play with.'

Daisy sullenly kicked a stone and, spotting Miranda, ran across the lawn. 'Want to play, Miranda?'

Miranda shook her head. 'I'm not in the mood for playing with piglets . . .'

'Richard . . . ?' Daisy bounded up on to the terrace and tugged at Richard's free hand.

'*Wir haben schön . . .*' Richard put his hand over Daisy's mouth to silence her and she bit it. 'Shit!' he yelled down the telephone.

Daisy giggled and went over to Christopher who was working on his computer. 'I'm bored,' she said. 'Nobody wants to play.'

'Sshh,' Christopher said. 'If you sit absolutely still and are absolutely silent for ten minutes I promise that I will play snakes and ladders with you.'

Ian gave a sigh of relief as Daisy pulled a chair up next to Christopher. 'All right,' he said. 'Let's start again.' He studied Lucy, noting the way her hair fell around the soft curve of her cheek and the dark intensity of her eyes. She had her mother's voluptuousness but, unlike Sarah, Lucy's was veiled by a certain sexual reserve. Ian hoped she wouldn't lose it.

Ian picked up his charcoal and sketch pad and

Lucy, in turn, was able to study him. He was wearing a rough cotton, navy blue shirt with the sleeves rolled up, and although the muscles in his arms were strong, his hands moved delicately over the paper. He was a very masculine man. And yet, she thought, there was an almost womanly sensitivity around his mouth and eyes.

'If this embarrasses you, tell me . . .' Ian put down the pad and pencil, leaned over and slipped one of the straps of Lucy's dress off her shoulder. 'I was thinking . . . ?'

Lucy was not only embarrassed but embarrassed about being so. She'd seen a drawing Ian had done of her mother, naked from the waist up, as well as the one of Miranda in the kitchen, and had been worrying, these last few days, that he might want her to pose semi-naked. She did hope he hadn't noticed her blushes. Anxious to appear sophisticated she slipped off the top of her dress. Artists were used to working with nude models, she tried to convince herself, it was perfectly natural. Anyway, she trusted Ian.

She pretended not to notice as Monseiur Guillaume walked down the lawn and took a chair in the shade, right next to them. He surveyed her with unabashed interest and then announced: 'Under this tree I inhabit that netherworld between life and art.' Lucy assumed he was being ironic, and supposed it was all right, him being there. After all, he was very old and obviously quite mad.

She was so taken up with thinking about Monsieur Guillaume and his outburst in the Pizzeria the

119

previous evening and trying not to think about Leonardo and how he'd pushed her out of his car, that she failed to notice Niccolo and Osvaldo on the terrace, gazing in her direction. Niccolo was doing more than gazing. He was staring at her with frank appraisal. 'A little young, but not bad,' he said, nudging Osvaldo in the ribs.

'The glasses are in here, boys,' Diana called out from the doorway.

Osvaldo shrugged and turned to go in.

'Oh, so you weren't looking?' said Niccolo, grinning.

'It's not appealing to me – girls who are unembarrassed in front of everyone,' Osvaldo said. 'Like a plastic person.'

Niccolo followed Osvaldo into the house. 'Yeah,' he said disbelievingly, 'Like you'd kick her out of bed.'

Richard, portable phone at his ear, was also watching Lucy. 'Hi there, I'm just calling in to see if you've got anything for me . . .' He looked around stealthily to see whether anyone was observing his interest. Miranda had vacated her vantage point on the lawn, Daisy and Christopher were engrossed in the laptop and Noemi appeared to be tying up bunches of dead flowers. Richard finished his call and gave Lucy his full attention. Those breasts! Wow! If only Miranda hadn't barged in. . . He turned around and there she was again, coming out onto the terrace, still looking bloody miserable. He turned hastily away from the garden and dialled another number. Miranda looked at him as though he wasn't there and, going over to Christopher, handed him a piece of paper. Boy, that woman could sulk. Richard was beginning to wonder if the game was worth the candle.

'What's this?' Christopher said taking the paper from Miranda. He glanced at it and raised a quizzical eyebrow.

'I found it on the path,' Miranda said, 'outside Lucy's room.' She lit a cigarette and hung over Christopher's shoulder as he typed: 'Hi, my name is Lucy. I'm eighteen. I'm a virgin. I wait, I wait so patiently . . . I'm quiet as a cup . . . I hope you'll come and rattle me . . . Quick, come wake me up!'

Daisy jumped up and tried to look. 'What is it? What is it?'

'Nothing that would interest you, Piglettina.' Christopher smiled sardonically at Miranda. 'Magic . . . pure poetry . . .'

'Oh, very pure,' Miranda said, not smiling back. A telephone rang inside the house and she started towards it, but was forestalled by Noemi, knocking over a chair in her hurry to get there first. Miranda picked up the chair. 'Well, Noemi is obviously expecting a call,' she said.

Noemi was hoping it would be Michele but had no intention of letting him know it. Her eyes were bright but her voice was cool as she said: 'Oh . . . Michele? Yes, well I'm not sure if I'm going tonight. No . . . I don't feel very social. Yes . . . I finished it . . . a little depressing . . . well, it is a depressing book . . .'

Out in the garden, Ian put down his charcoal,

stood up and stretched. 'If I'm not ready now, I never will be.' He smiled at Lucy. 'You are now free.' He picked up his pad and walked back towards the house. Lucy, rearranging her dress, saw that Niccolo had come out onto the terrace and was watching her. She looked back at him, doubtfully.

But, of course, when he asked her, after lunch, if she'd like to take a walk, she agreed without a second's hesitation.

They wandered down the driveway, passed Ian's studio and the busy sound of his buzz-saw, and walked in amongst the gnarled silver trees of an olive grove.

'So, where's Gabriella?' said Lucy, coming straight to the point.

'Gabriella?' said Niccolo, as though he was having difficulty remembering a girl named Gabriella. 'Oh . . . she left.'

'When?'

'This morning. I asked her to.'

'Why?'

Niccolo stopped walking and turned to face Lucy. 'Why do you think?' He paused and caressed her cheek. 'I wanted to see you . . .' His hand slid down to her breast, 'Lucy.'

She looked around . . . 'This is an olive grove, isn't it?'

'Of course.' Niccolo watched curiously as Lucy walked over to one of the olive trees, snapped off a leaf and chewed it. He decided to ignore her odd behaviour and followed her. 'You looked very beautiful back there . . . like this.' He slipped a strap over her shoulder. 'I could not take my eyes away.' He reached out to remove the other strap, but Lucy pulled away from him.

'No.' She'd spent years longing to be close to Niccolo; so why did it seem so important now to cling on to that strap?

Niccolo kissed her bare shoulder. 'I wanted to kiss you right here . . . and here . . .' He bent his head and kissed her covered breast. And then he bent lower and, through the thin cotton of her dress, pressed his face into her crotch. Straightening, he manoeuvred her up against the tree. 'I need to kiss your mouth, Lucy. Can I . . . after this long time?' He lifted her chin and kissed her more urgently and seriously then he had that time four years ago, by the lake.

As he kissed her, Lucy felt his hand move down past her waist and begin to lift her dress. She frowned and moved away; this was too obviously a repeat performance of the scene in the lemon grove. Taking Niccolo's hand, she led him into a thicket of trees and lay down.

Niccolo, encouraged and aroused by her apparent invitation, lay down beside Lucy and again attempted to pull down the top of her dress.

'No.' Lucy clung tenaciously to the remaining strap. Niccolo slowly let out his breath; was it pleasure or irritation? She couldn't tell. He lay on top of her, lifted her dress and reached between her legs. Lucy stared up at the twisted branches above her as she felt his hand move to her crotch. It seemed more like a violation than a caress. 'No.'

'God. That is . . . so lovely, Lucy.' Niccolo's voice thickened with emotion. 'I love feeling you.' Clumsily, he unzipped his trousers and pushed against her.

'No,' Lucy said. 'Wait.' This was too much . . . too soon.

Niccolo paused for only a second. 'Lucy. Won't you let me . . .? Don't you know I'm dying for you?'

She closed her eyes. She felt him move on top of her. She had dreamed of this moment so often and now it was happening and it was, somehow, terribly wrong. She stiffened. 'No, I can't,' she said. 'Not here.' Niccolo, ignoring her protests, continued to bear down on her. Lucy looked up and saw, to her horror, that she was not gazing into the eyes of a lover, but the uncaring eyes of a practised seducer. She tried hard to push him away. 'Niccolo . . . stop.' He tugged urgently at her briefs. 'I said stop.' Reaching out and grabbing his hand, she bent his fingers right back. Niccolo cried out in pain and drew up slightly. In that moment she scrambled to her feet, pulled up the strap on her dress and ran back towards the house, leaving Niccolo on the ground, nursing his sore fingers, and bruised ego.

Sobbing, Lucy hoped fervently to get back to her room without meeting anyone, but Alex was sitting outside the cottage attached to his IV, looking sick and weary. His face brightened when she came into view.

'Lucy. I want to know what you're wearing to the party tonight,' he said, and Lucy thought it would be rather nice to have a father like Alex; somebody who was actually interested in your fashion outfits and was also pretty good at talking about Life with a capital L.

Right now, though, she felt too distressed to talk and she hurried past him without answering. Standing in the middle of her room, she touched herself where Niccolo had touched her, and, her mind spinning, went over to the mirror and looked at her face searchingly, in conflict with herself, rubbing at the tears. All her dreams had been destroyed back there in the olive grove; she felt disillusioned, soiled. Trembling, she went to her duffle bag, searching for her mother's old journal. She drew it out and was opening it when Alex knocked on the door.

'Lucy?' He came in. 'What's the matter, love?'

Lucy leafed through the journal; it seemed right, somehow, to share its secrets with Alex. 'This was Mummy's,' she said, 'from right before she died. Listen. It's about me.'

Alex slumped down onto a chair as Lucy read slowly: '"Where have they gone, the green sandals? I was not made to be a mother. I had too stricken a heart, so I wore green sandals to stay apart. Then, one night, a man stood in an olive grove. He beat a viper till it bled, then drew me down low. I went farther than he'd ever know. One night was all there was. He fed me an olive leaf, then broke the strap of my dress. I kept on the green sandals. I could feel them in my throat, but I could not get off that hill. Italy, Italy, where did you take me that night so black and still? . . .'' Lucy choked on hot tears. 'Here,' she went and sat on the arm of Alex's chair and handed him the journal. 'You read the rest.'

Alex put an arm around her and continued reading, softly: 'He took the green sandals from me. He had an accent and a knife and somewhere even had a wife. He took my face and tore my hips and planted in their place something new and strange and near to love . . . I thought I had nothing left. But you came later, curved and new. Forgive me, I did not have the means for catching when I got, poor Lucy, you.' Alex didn't look up when he'd finished reading.

'It's about my father,' Lucy said. 'My real father.'

Alex lifted his eyes from the poem. 'It would seem so.'

She looked at him hopefully. 'It's not you, is it?'

'Can you imagine me beating a viper?' Alex said. 'I don't even know what a viper looks like.'

'It could be Carlo Lisca . . .'

'Good God . . .'

'But now I'm not sure. And I . . .'

Alex gave the journal back to Lucy and noticed, for the first time, that she seemed rather dishevelled. 'Has anything happened?'

'Well . . . I was with Niccolo . . .' It was such a relief to confide in someone. 'I thought . . . I thought I loved him. That letter he wrote. . . I don't know . . . I don't know what I'm doing.'

'Of course not,' Alex said. 'You've just read me why.'

'What does that . . . have to do with it?' Lucy said uncertainly.

'Everything. One leads directly to the other.'

'Then I should just forget about it. After all, I have a father already, who I love and—'

'Lucy, don't talk yourself out of your own curiosity. It's there to draw you through life.' Alex attempted a smile through thin lips. 'Although I must admit I would find it somewhat unnerving to discover Carlo Lisca was a relation.'

'I just want to know,' Lucy said vehemently.

'Naturally.' He closed his eyes.

Lucy looked at him anxiously. 'Alex?' He didn't reply and she repeated his name urgently, 'Alex?'

Slowly, and with an effort, he opened his eyes. 'Just feeling a bit . . . grotty . . . today . . . that's all.'

Lucy stood up, suddenly realising that Alex was desperately sick and here she was burdening him with her own pathetic worries. 'Can I get you . . . do you need a pill, or anything?'

'No, don't fuss. I'll be all right in a minute . . .' He paused and summoning a deep breath, spoke firmly. 'Don't give up, my darling Lucy. You'll find him. You must do that.'

CHAPTER NINE

Lucy lay in the bath, engulfed and protected by its warm vastness, and decided that this had probably been the longest day of her life. Was it only this morning that she had watched Leonardo's car disappearing over the hill and shared an espresso and a panoramic view of Siena with Michele? How she'd dreaded coming face to face with Richard after that cat stuff. Or with Miranda, for that matter. The way she'd looked at them when she'd found them licking the mirror; as though they were perverts, or something.

But they'd both kept out of her way. Richard making self-important international calls from the terrace, and Miranda marooned in the middle of the lawn. Later, before she'd gone off with Niccolo, Lucy had noticed them heading towards their bedroom. If Miranda's grim expression was anything to go by Richard would have been lucky to get anything more erotic than a siesta.

Lucy caught herself smiling as she slowly soaped the sponge. Smiling? Was she a totally shallow human being or what? How was it possible to find anything even vaguely funny when all her hopes had been so cruelly shattered? She'd wasted four years longing for Niccolo, sighing over his photograph, turning down great invitations from perfectly okay guys, and hinting to friends about a glamorous Italian lover, only to discover that she meant no more to him than a casual girl in a bright blue skirt. Why, he hadn't even remembered who she was . . .

She turned the hot tap on with her toe and, soothed by the steam, acknowledged the truth that her obsession with Niccolo had been a romantic dream; powerful but without substance. And, this afternoon, it had been exorcised.

She got out of the bath and, standing in front of the floor length mirror to dry herself, was surprised to find the reflection of her clean, untouched body curiously pleasing.

She switched her mind to the Donatis' party. The way everyone had been going on about it, it was obviously something very special. Lucy felt sure it would be packed with dauntingly sophisticated people who'd all known each other since childhood and she would be totally left out. She was desperately anxious to look like them, a woman of the world, rather than a naive teenager prone to bouts of shyness. To help achieve this unlikely persona she blow-dried her hair with considerable care and put it up. The effect was pretty good, as though she'd casually swept it on top of her head and stray tendrils had wilfully escaped to curl around her forehead and cling to the nape of her neck. Nobody, she thought, would guess that it had taken her ages and a lot of hairdressers' hardware to get it that way. She put on her mother's dress, and her last present – a pair of white river-pearl earrings. She slipped her feet into a pair of soft white leather pumps.

Carlo would probably be there tonight, and she was determined to question him closely. Perhaps, after all, he was the man who knew about the green sandals – the father she was hoping to find.

Passing through Ian's studio on her way to join the others, Lucy found him still working. 'Oh, sorry,' she said, backing out of the room. 'I didn't think anyone was here.'

Ian, a cigarette drooping from his lip, was carving with sure, clean strokes. 'It's okay, come through.' He glanced at Lucy in the long, white dress and quickly looked away again. 'Don't you look nice.'

Lucy, encouraged, came closer. 'Can I see?'

'*No.*' Startled, she turned to go, but Ian raised a hand and smiled apologetically. 'Sorry. I didn't mean to shout. It's just. . . I never let anyone see until it's done.'

'Does it look like me?' Lucy said uncertainly.

'It's not supposed to.'

'It's not?'

He grinned. 'No, it's like me. Didn't they teach you at college that the artist expresses himself? You're only the means through which I do it.'

Lucy laughed. 'Well . . . thanks.'

Just then Diana appeared in the doorway and said to Ian: 'Sure you won't come?'

'It's been the same every year,' he said. 'They won't miss me.' He walked to the door with Lucy, and watched the young woman and his wife walk out to the driveway together. He hoped with all his heart that Diana wasn't going to be hurt. She meant everything to him. Meeting her had been like coming home. He was much older than her, of course, but they'd been brought up on the same patch and had shared references from the past – the first gasps of cigarette smoke behind the boiler-house at St Joseph's Mixed Grammar, fumbled kisses in the Emerald Dance Hall, the old man who stood outside Mooneys, prophesying eternal damnation to the sinners about to partake of a couple of pints of Guinness on a Friday night. He went slowly back into his studio. Diana was not just his past. She was his present and his future. He couldn't imagine life without her.

Lucy and Diana joined the others, busily slotting into two cars to drive off to the Donatis' party. Christopher suddenly stopped and pointed across at the next hill. 'Jesus,' he said. 'Just look at that. It's going up.'

They turned to see the new television transmitter tower rising into the sky like a very slow space rocket. The sight filled Diana with doom; she looked around for Ian, for comfort, but he had gone back into his studio. Sadly, she followed Lucy into one of the cars.

Daisy could see her mother waving goodbye through the back window of the car as they all drove off down the drive. She hoped Mummy would notice that she was not waving back but pouting like one of those supermodels in the fashion magazines. She wasn't allowed to bother Daddy in his studio, so they'd left her in the charge of Maria, a girl from the village she didn't particularly like, anyway. Daisy didn't see why she couldn't go to the party, too. It was all jolly unfair.

Actually, she had a plan. She waited until Maria had disappeared into the kitchen to prepare her supper, and then ran quickly over to the cottage, and into Lucy's bedroom. Last time she'd been in there, talking to Lucy, she'd noticed a Video-8 tape in her duffle bag. It was Daisy's opinion that, apart from *The Wizard of Oz*, most grown-up movies were a lot more interesting than the boring stuff they put out for children, and she was curious to see whatever it was Lucy found so interesting that she carried it around with her.

It took Daisy quite a long time to find the tape because there was such a mess in the duffle, but eventually she got hold of it and, stuffing it into her knickers, returned to the house and the living room by way of the study, to avoid Maria who'd be sure to ask where she'd been.

She removed the tape, efficiently slotted it into an adaptor and then into the video and pressed the relevant buttons. Pulling up a chair she sat down to watch.

It was a really weird film of Lucy, obviously taken when she was arriving in Siena because she was on a plane and then she was on a train and

Daisy recognised the station. Only it didn't really look like Lucy. The camera seemed to be spying on her while she was asleep and there were horrible close-ups of bits of her. One with her mouth slightly open and spit dribbling down her chin; one with her hand hanging between the legs of her jeans in quite a rude way; another where the camera was practically diving down the front of Lucy's open-necked shirt.

Daisy didn't understand that it was a corruption of innocence, she just knew that she was watching something creepy and evil. When the film suddenly switched to what seemed to be newsreel of a war, with lots of pictures of dead and dying people, her expression didn't change.

The alley of cypress trees leading to the Villa Donati was illuminated by dozens of candles, outlining the branches against the setting sun and there was a distant throb of music. The Grayson party parked their cars and followed the procession of guests up to the house.

On the stage of an outdoor theatre, Lucy glimpsed the town band playing an old waltz. The musicians were wearing peaked caps and under one of them she could see Osvaldo fingering a clarinet. The stage was decorated with clumps of purple bougainvillea and swathes of glossy dark green ivy. 'God, look at that,' she said to Noemi. 'This is really something else.'

'Once a year Chiarella pushes out the boat,'

Noemi said. She wondered if Michele had arrived yet.

There was a ringing noise very close behind them and Lucy turned to see Richard reaching into his jacket pocket for his portable phone.

Miranda, next to him, rolled her eyes in exasperation. 'I can't believe you have actually brought that thing . . .'

'Take it away and you'd cut off his oxygen supply,' Christopher said.

Leaving Richard with his phone, Miranda caught up with Lucy. 'Darling,' she said, 'can I do you a favour?'

'What?' Lucy looked at Miranda suspiciously, but there seemed to be nothing but goodwill shining back from her expertly made-up brown eyes.

Miranda reached up and pulled out the pins and combs and bands with which Lucy had painstakingly created her hairstyle.

'Hey, wait a minute . . .' Lucy was thinking about getting really angry, but then she felt her hair tumbling down around her shoulders and it felt sort of comfortable and right. She guessed it must look that way, too.

'There,' Miranda said, 'it's better like that.'

'She's right, darling,' Noemi said. 'This is the best look for you.'

'Well . . . thanks.' Lucy recognised the gesture as the olive branch it was intended to be and smiled at Miranda, genuinely pleased. Miranda smiled back. She'd spent the afternoon grilling Richard about the strange scene she'd interrupted in Lucy's room and she knew exactly who had been responsible for the game of pussy-cats.

Diana was keeping Monsieur Guillaume company at the back of the group. 'My sister phoned me today, and told me she'd just met her first grandson,' she was saying. 'She said it was transcendent. Silly of me to feel homesick on such a magic night, isn't it?'

Monsieur Guillaume was fond of Diana. As he grew older the invitations had become sparser, friends had dropped away but Diana never seemed to notice that his hands had begun to shake and that he wasn't always able to say exactly what he meant. He took her arm – not, on this occasion for support – and squeezed it affectionately. 'Beauty wounds the heart, my dear.'

They arrived in the courtyard where Lucy had parked her bike so hopefully the previous day. The first person she saw in the crowd was Niccolo, arranging a young woman's hair over her shoulders with tender solicitude. Lucy waited for a pang of heartache, but it didn't come. She felt nothing but pleasure in the balmy air and wonder at the grandeur of the setting as Chiarella swept towards them in a magnificent black gown, arms outstretched. 'Darlings!'

'I'm glad you did it,' Diana said, kissing her. 'It wouldn't have been summer without your party.'

Chiarella embraced Diana and put an arm around Lucy's shoulders. 'Diana was here for the first one we had. And Sarah, too, wasn't she?' Diana nodded and smiled encouragingly at Lucy;

she hoped she wasn't upset by the frequent references to her mother. 'Well, I figure I always did the
planning, anyway,' Chiarella was saying. 'My hus-
band usually had a number of complaints about the
way I handled it. This year . . . no complaints. And
I've got a great surprise.'

She released Lucy who, seeing Carlo Lisca at the
other side of the courtyard, started to thread her
way through the crush towards him. By the time
she arrived he was deep in conversation with two
men. Lucy looked around for Osvaldo, the only
other person at the party she reckoned she'd know.
He was no longer on the stage but standing at the
side of a girl dressed in an elegant Italian manner –
she seemed to be quite a lot older than him. She
was smiling up at Osvaldo in a way which clearly
indicated, this is mine, so keep away.

Simultaneously, Osvaldo noticed Lucy, and was
irritated when Silvia, a friend of Niccolo's who
seemed to have attached herself to him, took his
arm. 'That was so nice,' she said admiringly.
'I'd love to play an instrument, but I have no
discipline.'

'Excuse me for a minute.' Osvaldo tried to pull
away as he saw Lucy disappearing into the crowd.
'I'll be right back.'

'Wait.' Silvia tightened her grip on his arm.
'Don't leave me alone. I don't know anyone here.'

Osvaldo looked around desperately. 'What about
Fiorella . . . and Gianni . . . and Mimo? And you
know the Ranuccis . . .'

'Well . . . hardly anyone,' Silvia said.

Lucy was now out of sight and a group of professional dancers had run out of the gallery, carrying flaming, flickering torches, transforming the garden into mysterious swirls and pools of light.

Diana clapped her hands in delight and turned to Chiarella. 'They're wonderful . . . delightful. Where did you find them?'

'In Montepulciano,' Chiarella said, gratified. 'Of course, you have to book them months in advance.'

Monsieur Guillaume, bemused by the noise and the music, pointed with a wavering finger towards a young man, arm in arm with one of the male dancers, who was trying to follow the jerky movements of their dance. 'Look,' he said. 'Over there. Isn't that . . . Christopher? What can he be doing?'

Before Diana could reply, the dancer, followed by Christopher, swooped up to them and placed a torch by their feet.

Diana was dismayed. The dancer was holding her son's arm in . . . well, she might as well admit it . . . in the caressing manner of a prospective lover.

'Sweetheart,' she said to Christopher, searching for the sort of innocuous question he could interpret as he pleased. 'Sweetheart, is this really what you want to do with your life?'

Christopher had, as it happened, already drunk four glasses of champagne and was incapable of taking in his mother's question, let alone placing any particular interpretation on it. He waved at her merrily and cavorted off after the dancer.

Diana sighed. She wasn't homophobic – at least, she didn't think she was – but it made her sad to think of Christopher missing out on children. It was her view that no matter how tiring and tiresome they could be, children – the propagation of the species – were what life was all about. Better not to think about it, she told herself and, squaring her shoulders, she took a firm grip of Monsieur Guillaume's arm. 'Come, Guy. Let's go and find something to eat.'

Lucy had, by now, drifted with the jostling crowd into a magnificent galleried hallway, decorated with rustic scenes and lined by tables laden with dishes of pasta and cold meats and salads: glazed suckling pigs and garnished whole salmon stared glassily at her from vast silver salvers.

She went over to look more closely at the frescos and Chiarella appeared at her side. 'I see you're admiring our frescos? You haven't been here before, have you?'

'Well . . . no,' Lucy said, not entirely truthfully. She found it really rather irritating that Chiarella Donati had chosen to come up and talk to her, now she no longer craved her approval.

Chiarella led Lucy over to a picture which depicted a hunting scene with the sun glinting through the trees, spotlighting the dogs and the wild boar and groups of muscular young men, and fashionably dressed young women with improbably high bosoms. 'This is the finest, I think. They were painted by Ignazio Moder at the end of the eighteenth century. Some of them need restoration but . . . in the present circumstances . . .' She left the sentence unfinished and shrugged expressively.

'They are very beautiful,' Lucy said, since Chiarella didn't seem to want to elaborate on what the present circumstances were.

'Your mother, too, found them beautiful. "Only an Italian could have conjured up colours of such subtlety," she said.' Chiarella gestured towards the food. 'Please help yourself . . . the plates are over there. I must go and make sure that the waiters are doing what I've paid them to do.' She patted Lucy's arm. 'Enjoy,' she said, and drifted away.

Lucy took a stalk of celery and, crunching contemplatively, decided that Chiarella was actually rather nice; thoughtful and serious, more like Osvaldo, really, than Niccolo. She wasn't feeling terribly hungry, and the reproachful eyes of a nearby honey-coated piglet did nothing to whet her appetite. Across the room Niccolo was chatting up another girl, feeding her a stalk of asparagus and whispering in her ear as she tilted her head and took the asparagus in her mouth in a frankly sexual manner. Lucy looked on recognising that the great love affair Niccolo enjoyed having again and again was with himself.

She was glad when there was a crackling noise in the sound system, followed by the loud, insistent beat of rock 'n roll. Chuck Berry, 'Sweet Little Sixteen', a number that invariably filled her with irrational happiness. She saw Carlo Lisca coming into the hall with a woman on each arm and went over to him. 'Do you want to dance?'

'Now?' Carlo said.

Lucy smiled at him. 'Now.'

139

Carlo shrugged and disengaged himself from his escorts, who stared at Lucy coldly. 'Okay.'

He led the way into the empty gallery and they started to dance. Osvaldo, standing by a doorway with Silvia, watched them morosely.

The tempo changed from Chuck Berry to the velvet smoothness of Nina Simone, and Carlo took Lucy into his arms.

'Michele says you're a liar,' she said. 'Is that true?'

'If I say, will I be lying?' Carlo said, holding her close.

'Do you remember where you were in August 1975?'

'I told you, I forget everything . . .' he paused and drew away slightly, 'actually, I do. That was after the fall of Saigon. Hard to forget the fall of Saigon.'

'But after?' Lucy said. 'Did you come back to Italy?'

'I don't think I ever came back,' Carlo said.

Other couples joined the dance floor, including the dancers from Montepulciano, holding their partners upside down so that their hair was almost sweeping the floor in spectacular fashion. Christopher, sipping a glass of champagne and swaying slightly, was watching them, enchanted.

'Did you see my mother around then?' Lucy said.

Carlo held her at arm's length. 'What is this? A quiz? A twenty questions? Lucy, your mother was not meant to be a married woman. When I met her she was already half out of it . . .'

'So, she was married when you met her?'

'Of course. Married women have always been my favourite.'

Lucy was beginning to realise that Carlo was a false trail and feeling rather pleased by this discovery, when a drunken middle-aged woman lurched in between them, pushing her face right up close to Lucy's.

'So, you're the new one?' she slurred. 'I'll show you what this bastard likes.' Lucy backed away as the woman squatted down in front of her, nearly falling over as she did so, lifted her skirt and peed on the floor.

Hardly anyone noticed, their attention having been diverted at the crucial moment by the professional troupe who were now dragging lagging guests onto the floor. Over the drunken woman's head, Lucy saw that one of them was Christopher.

'Marta, what the fuck are you doing?' Carlo said amiably, and tried to pull Lucy away, but the woman had a firm grip on her leg.

Lucy ought to have been disgusted, but somehow she wasn't. So many strange things had happened to her in the last few days that she had begun to feel incapable of any sort of complex emotional response; she had become a blank canvas upon which other people made their mark. She'd always been a bit like that, anyway. Her friend Lizzie, who was in the same year at college, had urged her towards empowerment. 'What personal goals are you working towards this semester, Lucy?' Lucy hadn't liked to admit that the only personal goal she'd been able to think of was to get her legs waxed regularly.

Getting no reply from Marta, Carlo let go of Lucy's arm and danced off by himself, leaving her to help the woman to her feet and pick up her handbag. She then swerved off into an empty room, supported by Lucy, and made straight for a table piled with leftover glasses. Helping herself to the fullest glass, she collapsed heavily onto a couch, tugging at her bra and adjusting her skirt. Lucy gave her the handbag.

'Who are you, anyway?' Marta snatched the bag defensively. 'You look vaguely familiar.'

'I'm staying with the Graysons,' Lucy said.

'God, more English.'

'No, American.'

'You're all over the place, too.' Marta reached out for another glass. 'It excites him to see a woman degraded, you see. He's got so jaded he's lost all normal feeling; he has to have the extra stimulation.' She drained the glass. 'I must be sick to want him. That's what you're thinking, isn't it?'

'No.' Lucy noticed that Marta's make-up was slapped on like stucco, there were smudges of lipstick on her chin.

She studied Lucy with drunken truculence. 'What the fuck do you know, anyway? You look like you're about twelve.' She rummaged through her handbag and finally came up with a packet of photographs. 'Here, you might learn something. This is what he used to like – pictures. Now it's the

142

video gets him going.' She held out the photographs.

'That's okay,' Lucy said, shaking her head.

'Afraid to soil your pretty little mind?' Marta taunted, challenging Lucy to take the pictures. Lucy glanced disinterestedly at them and tried to give them back, but Marta ignored her outstretched hand and returned to the table in search of another glass. 'It must be on film, otherwise it's not real enough.'

Lucy sat down and flicked through the photographs which featured dead-eyed people doing unpleasant things to other people with ropes and whips and chains.

'For him there is no perversion possible in sex,' Maria said, scooping up a number of half empty glasses and pouring them into the one in her hand. 'It is the only time when everything . . . anything . . . is allowed.'

Riffling through, Lucy came to a photograph of a threesome on a bed. One of the women looked like a younger Marta, the man was young and black, the other woman was wearing a mask. Lucy put her hand over the masked head, considering the woman's body. She hoped she was not, as she suspected, looking at her mother's naked breasts, but she kept the picture, anyway, and slipped it under the chair cushion.

'You'll try it some day, if you're lucky,' Marta said. She laughed joylessly. 'If he knew I was showing you these I would get a bad spanking.' She put the pictures back in her bag and made unsteadily for the door. 'And now I need a *real* drink.'

Lucy retrieved the photograph, tucked it down the front of her dress and went out into the garden. She felt she could do with some cleansing fresh air. Niccolo passed by, playfully sharing a slice of watermelon with the asparagus eater and behind them Lucy could see Noemi and Michele reaching out to take champagne from a passing tray. She went towards them. Noemi, beautiful in a silk sweater worn over something ice-green and slightly see-through, was looking mettlesome. Michele seemed confused. They were talking intensely in Italian which, Lucy thought, was a good language to be intense in. She realised they were discussing the book which Noemi had received with such lack of enthusiasm.

'What I don't understand,' Noemi was saying, 'is why you give me a book about a young man who completely destroys an older woman who loves him?'

'But it's so truthful,' Michele insisted. 'I can identify myself with him, exactly—'

'Excuse me,' Noemi cried, tossing back her long auburn curls in a challenging manner. 'Am I hearing you right? You identify with this man who couldn't care less about the woman who has given him everything?'

'No, no,' Michele said anxiously, 'that's not what I meant at all . . .'

Lucy watched as Michele followed Noemi into a

144

small outhouse and shut the door behind them. Then she wandered back into the house.

'Look at you,' Michele said, 'how you're standing.'

Noemi had led him into a room stacked with dusty barrels of wine and although she was barely visible in the shade of one of the barrels, he could see that she had her arms firmly crossed in a defensive manner. How he wished he'd never given her that wretched book.

'How? How am I standing?'

'What are you so afraid of?' Michele said softly. 'What did men ever do to you that was so bad?'

'Nothing.' Noemi uncrossed her arms. 'Nothing. You don't want to know.'

'I want to know everything about you,' Michele said, truthfully. He moved towards her.

'What are you doing?'

Michele kissed her neck. 'Do you mind?' Noemi didn't move. 'I won't hurt you, I promise.'

Noemi fell against him as he kissed her mouth. He felt the depth of her response and then she suddenly pulled away. 'You won't be able to help it,' she said sadly.

Michele watched her walk towards the door. He felt sure that she was leaving him but, at the last moment, she stopped and pulled down one of the sleeves of her sweater. Looking over her bare shoulder she smiled at him and, flinging off the sweater, ran out into the garden in her shiny, transparent skirt. She pulled off one high-heel and threw it towards him, and then the other. Michele thought that she was irresistibly tantalising. He picked up the sweater, caught the shoes and came swiftly after her as she ran towards the terrace wall, unzipping her skirt. An arc of silk floated through the dim light of the garden.

Osvaldo and Silvia sat on the edge of the terrace swinging their legs and eating olives.

'You've changed since we last met,' Silvia said, shifting closer to Osvaldo. 'I didn't recognise you at first, you have become so grown-up.'

Osvaldo moved slightly away from Silvia and passed her another olive. 'You are just the same,' he said enigmatically. He'd never liked Silvia much and he liked her even less this evening, for keeping him away from Lucy.

Silvia bit the olive thoughtfully. Was this a compliment or a criticism? She spat out the stone, and somebody below called out in Italian, 'Hey. Stop it.'

Osvaldo thought he recognised Michele's voice. He launched another exploratory olive stone. It was definitely Michele who shouted back: 'What on earth's going on up there?'

'I think, perhaps we should go,' he said. 'We seem to be bombarding a friend of mine.' He helped Silvia to her feet and, as she bent to straighten her dress, he disappeared swiftly into the dusk.

Lucy was sauntering along one of the many long corridors in the Donati villa when she saw a shaft of light beaming out from an open doorway. She stepped into a billiard room. The party had thinned out, but there was still an air of enthusiastic dissipation. A few people she didn't know were shooting pool. In one corner Chiarella, Monsieur Guillaume and Diana were deep in conversation; another group, including Richard and Miranda, were swaying gently to one of Stevie Wonder's slower, sexier numbers.

'You look as though you've lost something,' somebody said in a slurred English accent. Just inside the door Lucy saw a young man in a green shirt, lolling in an armchair.

'I haven't lost anything,' she said.

'Perhaps I can help you find it.' The young man rose unsteadily to his feet.

She smiled at him. 'Do you have a cigarette? I'm Lucy.'

'Gregory,' the young man said and sat down again quickly. 'Will a cigar do?'

'Please.' Lucy took the cigar and as Gregory struck a match and lit it, Monsieur Guillaume, followed by Diana, Miranda and Richard passed by. As they went out of the door, they turned and looked curiously at Lucy and Gregory. Diana signalled that she was leaving and, raising her eyes, gave a little nod, which Lucy understood to mean: hmm, not bad . . .

'Do you ever get the feeling you're being watched?'

Gregory nodded. At that moment he realised that a girl was actually staring at him with her head upside down. A group of dancers were now in the centre of the room performing the floor-sweeping number with the women's hair. Lucy noticed that Christopher was amongst them, dancing rather ineptly by himself. Gregory shook his head, not quite believing what he was seeing, and focused on the nice girl smoking his cigar. 'Come and sit down,' he said, moving up to make room for her.

He put a tentative arm around Lucy's shoulders as she perched next to him on the chair; she seemed chilled by the evening air. 'Here,' he said, struggling out of his jacket and putting it around her, 'this'll warm you up.'

Lucy sat hunched in the jacket, watching the dancers and puffing at the cigar, which made her feel a bit queasy. Gregory was speaking. She concentrated on what he was saying . . .

'You see, the Stewarts are famous for their drinking. They can drink more than anyone I know. They're always the life and soul of the party and then suddenly they disappear. And that's what they've done – I've been completely abandoned.'

'So you're the one who's lost something,' she said.

'The point is,' Gregory said, trying desperately to remember what the point was, 'the point is that I don't have the faintest idea where I'm staying. Down some winding little road and then up some winding little hill, so far as I can remember.' He looked at Lucy helplessly. 'I don't even remember where I am now. Where are we?'

A vague idea was forming at the back of Lucy's mind, which, she hoped, would finally satisfy the curiosity about who she was going to sleep with. 'You can stay with me,' she said. 'It's near here.'

'Really?' Gregory looked at her, as if for the first time. 'How awfully nice of you. I can give us a lift.'

Lucy and Gregory left the house together and went down the path through the garden where a group of young people, Osvaldo included, were involved in an improvised guitar session. Osvaldo jumped up. He'd only just found Lucy and now she appeared to be leaving with somebody else. He noticed gloomily that she was wearing a man's jacket. 'Wait.' He grabbed her wrist. 'You're not going?'

'Yes,' Lucy said. 'Why?' She waved at Christopher, who passed by them with one of the dancers.

'I just . . . no, it's okay . . . well, goodnight . . .' Osvaldo stood looking at Lucy uncertainly.

'No, what?' Lucy said.

'Nothing . . .' Osvaldo said, 'I wanted to ask you something . . .'

'Yes?' Lucy turned back.

'Well, I wanted to ask you. . . I was thinking of going to America and was wondering if you knew of any . . . you know, places to stay, and getting a job. If you knew about that.' Osvaldo finished the sentence in a rush.

Lucy looked up at Gregory, she hoped he wouldn't run away. 'Yeah. Well, maybe later,' she said. 'I could probably tell you some things . . . before I leave.'

'When?' Osvaldo said eagerly, grabbing her wrist again.

149

'Tomorrow?' Lucy said, releasing her wrist. 'Maybe tomorrow.'

'Okay,' Osvaldo said, 'I'll come over tomorrow.' He nodded at Gregory who had moved away from them and was doing a strange solitary dance in time to the music. 'Are you sure he can drive?'

Gregory jigged up to them. ' 'Course I can drive.' He took Lucy's arm. 'Come on.'

Without looking back at Osvaldo, Lucy called out: 'Oh, by the way, thanks for the party. Thanks.'

'Yes, wonderful party . . .' Gregory propelled Lucy firmly across the courtyard, passing Marta and Carlo locked in a tortuous embrace and shouting obscenities. As Gregory opened his car door Lucy was not totally surprised to see a couple disentangle themselves from the back seat and climb out. Gregory didn't even notice them.

The car pulled up in front of the Graysons' house in a cloud of dust. Gregory put on the brake, switched off the lights and then slumped over the driving wheel, relieved to have survived the journey. Lucy got out and, looking up at the lights of the house, noticed Diana in her evening dress watching her from the studio window, with Ian by her side.

She opened the driver's door and pulled Gregory out. He stood unsteadily next to her. Lucy embraced him. 'Hug me,' she said. Gregory put his arms around her. 'Now,' she whispered, 'kiss me.' Gregory kissed her.

They walked unsteadily together along the terrace. 'Sshh,' Gregory murmured, holding on to

Lucy for support. 'Absolutely no kissing, no. Because I am, above all, an Englishman and a gentleman . . .'

Lucy glanced up at Christopher's window. Beside him appeared the silhouette of a dancer, who looked to Lucy vaguely like a lissom young man. She stopped briefly and gave Gregory an affectionate hug.

Richard and Miranda had just started undressing when they heard muted voices outside the bedroom. Richard stepped out to investigate and saw Lucy embracing Gregory under the portico.

'Grab my ass,' Lucy whispered to Gregory. She suspected that Richard was there, watching.

'No kissing . . .' Gregory murmured, clumsily leaning against Lucy and placing his hands around her backside. 'No kissing.'

'Hey babe,' Richard called out to Miranda, 'come here for a second. Get this . . .' Miranda came and looked. Richard grabbed her and tried to kiss her. 'I like it when you're mad . . .'

Miranda twisted out of his grasp. 'No, Richard. No.'

'Come,' Lucy whispered to Gregory, leading him towards the cottage.

Gregory followed Lucy into her room. He had a feeling that some sort of explanation was in order. 'I know how it looks,' he said. 'They are wonderful, wonderful friends, really. They just have this strange habit of disappearing, which means, as usual, I've been completely abandoned . . .' He sat down heavily on the bed.

Lucy took off the jacket and handed it to him. 'I won't be long,' she said.

'Good,' Gregory fell back on the bed. 'Right.'

Lucy walked up and down outside Alex's room. Was it because she was a bit drunk, or was she right in thinking that he'd want to know about Gregory? She knew Alex was fond of her; sometimes she'd even thought he fancied her, which was pretty odd considering that he was really quite old and desperately ill. She didn't want to disturb him if he was asleep, but she had a funny feeling he was waiting for the end of her story, as though it was the final page of the play he would never, now, be able to write. She tapped gently on his door. Okay, she had no intention of sleeping with Gregory, he was probably out cold by now, anyway, but Alex wasn't to know that.

Alex heard the tap and saw Lucy's shadow moving behind the door. He had not been asleep but had been searching, with painful excitement, through his bookshelves, anxious to find a particular book. He put his hand to his head and winced. Swiftly putting on his knitted helmet he called out: 'Come in.'

Lucy entered the room: 'Hi . . .'

Alex guessed what she was going to say; it pleased him that Lucy had chosen to confide in him, but he wished, ruefully, that he could have been more to her than a sympathetic confidant. 'Hi,' he said.

'So, I brought someone back with me.'

'I heard the heavy tread,' Alex said. 'Who's the lucky fellow?'

Lucy shrugged. 'Just a guy from the party.'

'Italian?'

'English, actually.'

Alex smiled. 'Oh, English . . .' He moved away from the bookshelf, winced with pain and said, with an effort, 'Good. I'm proud to be so close on such an auspicious occasion.'

'Are you okay?' Lucy said.

'Don't worry about me.' He turned back to the bookshelf. 'I don't like it, you know.'

'I'm not,' she lied. 'What are you doing?'

'I've lost something,' Alex said, 'and I think it might be one of the best things I've ever written.' He began feverishly hunting along the shelf again. 'Of course, I would think that since I can't find it.' There was a long pause while he searched. 'Go on,' he said eventually, studying the bookshelf, not able to look at her. 'Off you go.'

'Right, then.' She waited anxiously, seeking his approval. 'Goodnight . . .' She moved slowly towards the door.

'Off you go,' he muttered again.

Lucy turned back to him. 'What?'

'Nothing,' Alex said. He waved as she left the room and closed the door. 'With you . . .' he murmured ironically, 'in spirit.'

Next door, Gregory was fast asleep on the bed still wearing his green shirt. Lucy quietly undressed and slipped into her long T-shirt. She pulled one of the pillows and a blanket off the bed as cautiously as she could but Gregory opened his eyes and gazed at her in bewilderment. 'Where are we?' he said. 'What are you doing?'

Lucy took the blanket and pillow over to the wooden couch. 'Going to sleep,' she said.

He attempted to rise. 'No ... course not. I'll absolutely sleep there ...' He fell back on his pillow. 'Oh, spinny head ...'

'It's okay,' Lucy said, 'be my guest.'

'No,' Gregory said. 'I absolutely insist ...' He fell back on the pillow and began snoring.

Miranda had taken off her dress and was sitting at the dressing table brushing her hair when Richard came up behind her.

She recognised the look in his eye. 'No, Richard.' She raised the hairbrush. 'No.'

Richard twisted the brush out of her grasp and forced her towards the bed. He flung her down and frenziedly tore at her bra and pants and ripped off her tights.

Miranda turned her face away, but her body responded as he stripped her and entered her. 'Now, tell me you don't like it,' Richard said.

Christopher was almost pirouetting around his room, gradually getting closer and closer to the dancer he'd brought home. Eventually, they embraced and fell together, entwined on the bed. As they started making love the canopy swung rhythmically and the legs of the bed scraped vigorously against the wooden floor boards.

Ian, dusty from work, turned towards Diana. In her evening clothes she seemed youthfully expectant, suffused with the excitement of the party. He walked around her, studying her. Diana stepped towards a statue and, leaning back against it, deliberately, provocatively, pulled up her skirt. They embraced and Ian slipped his hand between her legs . . .

Out in their pen, even the peacocks were mating. Lucy, alone on the couch in the middle of the night and unable to sleep, heard them in the far distance. She lit another cigarette and stared sorrowfully at the ceiling.

CHAPTER TEN

Gregory woke to the sound of gushing water. He opened his eyes and immediately closed them against the bright sunlight. He lay there, worried. Was he imagining it, or had he just seen a girl in a T-shirt darting behind a screen in the middle of his room?

Lifting his head from the pillow he looked cautiously around. The girl came out from behind the screen to collect a towel and Gregory studied her carefully. She looked an awfully pleasant girl. He wondered who she was and whether he had behaved appallingly badly towards her. He coughed to alert her to the fact that he was awake. She came over to him, her towel slung over her shoulder. 'Last night . . . ?' he ventured.

'You were abandoned at the Donatis' party, so I brought you back with me,' she said.

Gregory sat up slowly and eased his legs out of the bed. He sat there shaking his head and rubbing his eyes for a moment. As he looked down at the swaying floor, he observed that he was still wearing his shirt and his trousers. He found this discovery reassuring. 'And . . . last night? I mean everything was okay, was it?'

'The perfect English gentleman.' She grinned at him. 'You're a great kisser.'

Gregory groaned. 'Oh God, I am most awfully sorry.'

'Nothing to be sorry about. Hey, let's start again from the top. My name is Lucy and I'm staying with some friends called the Graysons who will be expecting us for breakfast very soon.'

Gregory's eyes widened in horror. 'No problem,' Lucy said reassuringly. 'They're very casual and they adore meeting new people.' She gathered her clothes and disappeared behind the screen.

After a bath, and an indifferent shave with Lucy's Lady Gillette, Gregory looked and felt a lot better. 'Are you sure this is going to be all right?'

Lucy took his hand. 'Come on, I'm starving.' Late nights usually made her want to eat vast quantities of food the following day. She raised a finger to her lips as they passed Alex's room. 'Ssh . . .' Tiptoeing over to the little window, she could see him lying on the bed, waxy and ashen-faced. His eyes were closed and his knitted cap was on the table; his head looked bare and vulnerable.

'What . . . ?' Gregory attempted to look inside the room, too, but Lucy held him back.

'No.' She didn't want him to see Alex; not like that.

In the kitchen Diana was cutting bread, staring at each slice in a sort of daze before slotting it into the toaster. Daisy was playing outside. Diana called her in to breakfast and then saw Lucy and Gregory coming across the terrace.

Lucy led Gregory into the kitchen. 'Morning, Diana. This is Gregory.'

Diana was pleased to see that the young man looked just as wholesome in the morning as he'd looked at the Donatis' party the previous evening. 'Good morning, Gregory, Would you . . . ah . . . like some coffee?'

'Yes,' Gregory said, sitting down. 'Thank you.'

Ian, entering the kitchen with a spring in his step, looked curiously at Gregory.

'Gregory . . .' Diana said, pouring coffee and retrieving toast.

'Right.' Ian pulled out a chair and picked up the local paper. 'How do you do? Morning Lucy – you're nearly finished.'

'Morning,' Lucy said.

'Coffee, sweet?' Diana hovered solicitously over Ian with the pot.

'Yes, yes,' said Ian, who was studying Gregory from behind his newspaper.

Miranda and Richard were next into the kitchen. Miranda had a brisk no-nonsense look about her, Richard seemed even more pleased with himself than usual. Gregory was reminded of that Marx Brothers film where more and more people keep pouring into the ship's cabin; there seemed to be a cast of thousands in this house.

'Who's this?' Miranda sat down and looked frankly at Gregory.

'Gregory,' Lucy said. 'Gregory, Miranda.'

Miranda smiled around at the room at large. 'Has Gregory won the lottery, then?'

Diana gave her daughter a warning frown. 'Miranda.'

'Not me,' Gregory said, 'I never win contests.'

Richard leaned over the table and grabbed Gregory's hand. 'Pleased to meet you. Richard Reed. Morning, Lucy.'

Lucy ignored Richard's greeting but Gregory shook his hand. 'Gregory,' he said.

Christopher cautiously edged his way into the kitchen and over to the cereal packets, acknowledging the stranger with a nod before taking his place at the table. Aldo, the dancer, had crept out of his room in the early dawn. Christopher hoped nobody had witnessed his departure.

Just when Gregory had decided that the Grayson ménage must surely be at full strength, a beautiful woman in a crumpled silk skirt and a sweater came in through the terrace door.

'Well, if it isn't Cinderella,' Miranda said.

Noemi, who enjoyed making an entrance, paused in the doorway. 'Morning all.' She swept the kitchen with a radiant smile which came to rest on Gregory. 'But I don't know you. Hullo.' She came towards him with an outstretched hand. 'I'm Noemi.'

'Pleased to meet you,' Gregory said. 'Gregory.'

'You're Lucy's friend?'

'From last night. She very kindly rescued me.'

'How nice,' Noemi said. 'Wasn't it fun? Didn't everyone have a really good time?'

Everyone looked blearily at Noemi; nobody replied.

Diana had to hold Alex's head so that he could drink through the straw. If she slackened her hold for a second he fell back against the pillows, pitifully weak. Diana choked back a mixture of tears and anxiety, she longed desperately to keep Alex with them, she couldn't bear the idea of losing him. Alex had been part of her life ever since they'd met at university, supporting her with love and advice throughout her gloomy marriage to Simon and enthusiastically acting the part of best man when she married Ian. He'd spent the summer with them in Tuscany ever since. Years ago, after a glorious rampage around the bars of Lucca and San Gimignano, they'd christened themselves The Terrible Trio. And now, Diana thought miserably, there would be only two of them, and neither of them, these days, up to much rampaging. She put the mug and the straw on the bedside table and gently lowered Alex's head onto the pillow. 'I'm going to have to call Doctor Signorelli, you know.'

'No.' Alex tried to shake his head but couldn't quite manage it. 'He smells like rotton meat. Can't bear it.'

Diana stroked his forehead. 'Alex, you need more help, darling.'

'I'm all right,' he muttered.

'We can't do enough for you here.'

There was the tiniest spark in Alex's eyes as he said: 'How's Lucy?'

'She's fine.'

'So, she chose a good one?'

Diana attempted a smile. 'Well . . . she chose her first one.'

'I'm glad. 'Oh God . . .' He squeezed her hand against the pain. 'It's ludicrous, isn't it? I'm about to snuff it . . . and I still . . .'

'. . . still want her,' Diana said. 'I know.'

Richard had gone upstairs to change into his white Adonis swimming briefs. He hadn't liked the way Miranda had followed; purposeful firm steps on the stairs behind him. And now she stood with her back to the door with the sort of expression on her face that meant It's Time We Had A Serious Talk. It reminded him of his mother when he was fifteen and had stayed out late three nights running without doing his homework.

'This is it,' Richard,' Miranda said.

So, he thought, I read the look aright. 'What are you talking about, sweetheart?'

'Us,' she said. 'This is it. I've had enough. *Finis.*'

'Enough?' Richard replied, bravely but foolishly. 'I haven't noticed it. Seems to me you've been getting what you want when you want it.'

'I see. I'm supposed to be grateful.' Miranda breathed in deeply, flaring her nostrils at him as if he was the wrong coloured bead in one of her necklaces.

'You are so out of it, Richard. It's breathtaking, really.'

'Excuse me.' He came towards her. 'Have I misled you in some way? So far as I'm concerned, it has always been what you see is what you get.'

'And I don't like what I see.'

'Oh, come on . . .' He reached out towards her. 'This isn't you. I know you.'

Miranda backed away. 'Know me?' she said bitterly. 'You know nothing about me. You've only ever looked into my eyes to see your own reflection.'

Richard shrugged. If that's how she wanted to play it. He took his leather suitcase – a Gucci copy marked down at Barney's – from the top of the cupboard, put it on the bed and started to pack. Come to think of it, there had been several times in the past few weeks when Miranda had sounded more like a nagging wife than Jeannie had ever done. Maybe he'd call her up when he got back to New York, see how she was fixed. He put his carefully folded shirts into the case and slipped his portable phone into an outside pocket.

Miranda watched him with tears in her eyes. Richard wasn't sure, and no longer felt inclined to enquire, whether they were tears of sorrow or of rage.

Miranda's car swerved around the lemon grove and accelerated off down the driveway. Lucy and Gregory, standing by Gregory's car, stepped smartly back to avoid the shower of stones and dust as it passed them.

They stood in front of each other, smiling diffidently. 'So . . . thank you,' Lucy said.

'Right,' Gregory laughed and half-cuffed, half-caressed her face gently with his fist. 'Right, then.'

He got into the car and then wound down his window and looked out. 'Thank you for what . . . exactly?'

'Nothing.'

'Right.'

'Bye.'

'*Ciao.*'

Gregory was still waving as he turned into the driveway, narrowly missing a sleek white car crossing the lemon grove on its way to the cottage. Lucy knew it was Dr Signorelli's car, she'd seen it before. She hurried back into the house in search of Daisy.

'He dreads the hospital,' Diana said to Dr Signorelli. They were walking back to the doctor's car after visiting Alex. Diana still nursed a vain hope that the doctor would tell her that this was only a temporary relapse and that Alex would be better left in her care.

Dr Signorelli put a comforting arm around her shoulders. 'They can help him there. Now it's just a question of managing the pain.' Suddenly he jumped away from Diana and started agitatedly swatting the air. 'Watch out! A bee!'

'Ignore it,' said Diana, who'd been ignoring Ian's bees for years. 'It won't sting you if you leave it alone. When? I mean, the ambulance . . . ?'

'Later on this morning.' Dr Signorelli, ashamed of his unprofessional behaviour over the bee, stopped waving his arms and spoke in a tone of brisk efficiency. 'Midday. Precisely.'

Diana saw the doctor to his car and then went over to the studio to find Ian. He was chiselling the final touches to Lucy's face and half-singing, half-mumbling an old Irish ballad about O' somebody or other's flute. Diana watched him affectionately, not wanting to spoil his obvious contentment, the result, she felt sure, of the previous night's rare and liberating passion. She went quietly over to the platform behind him and sat down.

Ian continued chiselling, anxious to postpone the moment when he knew he'd have to hear the terrible news he could sense she was aching to share. But when, eventually, no longer able to contain her tears, she jumped up and hugged him, he put his arms around her and held her close.

'He's got to go . . .' Diana sobbed, 'he's got to go.'

Dr Signorelli had been right. It was 12.02 precisely when the two ambulance men carried Alex out of the cottage. They were followed by Diana and Daisy. Diana, walking by Alex's side, held a straw hat above his face to protect him from the sun. Daisy was accompanied by her friend and comforter, a rag doll called Mr Jones.

Ian, Noemi, Michele, Christopher and Monsieur Guillaume stood about on the lawn, wanting to help and say the right things and not entirely certain how to go about it.

Alex was looking rather better than he had done at breakfast time. Diana wondered if, secretly, he was relieved to be going where nothing would be expected of him, where he wouldn't have to pretend any more. He turned his head on the stretcher. 'Oh, give me a ciggie, Ian.'

'For God's sake, Alex,' Ian said, with what he hoped sounded like humour, 'when was the last time you bought a cigarette?'

'Last time you bought a decent shirt,' Alex replied. He started singing: 'Goodbye-ee, goodbye-ee . . .' in a brave quavering voice but, suddenly catching sight of Noemi, stopped in mid-chorus. 'Noemi . . .'

'Alex . . .' Noemi, summoning a smile, rushed to his side and took his hand.

'It's all the doctor's fault. I'm really perfectly capable of walking, you know.' The ambulance men laid the stretcher carefully down on the ground and opened the doors of the ambulance. Alex grinned at Daisy. 'It's like being in a parade, isn't it?'

Daisy waved Mr Jones's hand at him, as if to say goodbye.

As they began loading Alex into the ambulance, Monsieur Guillaume, choking, put his hand on Michele's arm. 'It ought to be me. I'm too old. I should be in his place.' Michele patted the hand, muttered something non-committal and put a consoling arm around Noemi.

Just before he disappeared inside the ambulance, Alex lifted his head and, still trying to make light of the pain and contain the knowledge that he would probably never see his friends again, said wryly: 'If only you could see yourselves.'

Lucy, who had been watching from behind one

of the terracotta figures, ran towards the ambulance and whispered to Diana, 'I don't want to see him at the hospital.'

'That's fine,' Diana said. 'You stay here. Just say goodbye.'

Lucy climbed into the ambulance where Alex was lying, slotted along one of the sides, covered in a red blanket. 'Let me look at you,' he said weakly. 'See if you look different . . .'

Lucy began, 'I didn't really, you know . . .' but Alex wasn't listening.

'You mustn't mind me . . .' His voice was so weak that Lucy had to bend down to hear what he was saying. 'I've loved watching . . . you . . . and haven't we all been lucky . . . to see such beauty . . .'

His voice trailed away and Lucy, flinging herself down next to the stretcher, put her arms around him and kissed him on the lips. She took a joint, tied with a red ribbon, out of her pocket. 'Take this with you.'

Alex smelled it and tucked it behind his ear. 'There's . . . my God . . . I'll share it with the nurses . . .'

Lucy kissed him again. 'See you.' Stumbling out of the ambulance, sobbing, she ran to her room.

From the window she watched the ambulance moving off down the driveway, taking Alex away from her. It didn't matter that he didn't know what a viper looked like, that he wasn't, after all, her father. He'd understood her. Dad was wonderful, of course, but she couldn't imagine smoking pot with him, discussing her sex life with him, telling him about Niccolo, the way she'd been able to talk to Alex. In a very short time she'd come to rely on Alex and love him. She knew he was going to die and found it strange that she grieved for him more than she had grieved for her mother. Lucy felt awful just thinking about how she'd felt after her mother had died. Sarah had always been an elusive presence, too absorbed in her own interests and desires, to accept the responsibility of a child. She had never been there for Lucy when she needed her, and killing herself had seemed to Lucy to be her mother's final act of selfish abandonment. Lucy's head drooped onto her folded arms and she wept, aware that she cried both for Alex and for the mother she'd never had.

CHAPTER ELEVEN

It was mid-afternoon and Lucy was sitting on Alex's unmade bed, still rumpled and slightly warm from his body, which made her feel that he hadn't gone away after all. She had her journal on her knee and was writing a poem. 'The die is cast,' she wrote . . . 'The dice are rolled . . . I feel like shit . . . You look like gold.' She tore the page out of the journal, hid it inside Eliot's *The Wasteland*, one of her favourite books, and slipped it under Alex's pillow. On the windowsill was his tray, holding a cup with a straw in it, a plate of uneaten toast and honey, medicine bottles, and wads of cotton wool. She got off the bed, straightened the covers and picked up the tray. Practical tasks to stop her thinking about the reality of what had happened that morning.

She'd just stepped out of the cottage when there was a horrendous buzzing sound. Several bees – it seemed to Lucy like a mass attack – were dive-bombing her face and neck. She felt a sharp sting and the tray went crashing to the ground as she put up her arms to protect herself.

Osvaldo, who'd been going through the house looking for Lucy, came out onto the terrace at that moment, and saw her flailing her arms, ducking her head and screaming. He rushed over.

'Ouch! Fuck!' she cried, still flailing.

Osvaldo whipped off his jacket and threw it protectively over her head. 'Come. Come with me.'

Once away from the bees, he removed his jacket, took Lucy's hand, and led her through a vineyard towards a small spring in a hollow between the slant of the hills. There, he gouged out a handful of mud from the edge of the water. 'Where did they get you?'

'Here.' Lucy pointed to her upper arm. 'Here.' She pointed to her neck. She wondered what on earth he was doing.

Osvaldo rubbed some of the mud on her arm and on her neck. 'This clay is good for you. It draws out the poison. Are you okay?'

'I'm not dying.' Lucy pulled back her shirt and rubbed the top of her chest. 'And here.'

Osvaldo picked up some more mud and hesitated. He looked at the swell of Lucy's breast. It was too much for him. He handed her the mud and said shyly, 'Here, you'd better . . .' and watched raptly as she smeared it on.

Miraculously, the stinging disappeared. Lucy stepped away from Osvaldo and then looked back. 'Come on, let's walk.'

They strolled together, in silence, across a rocky promontory and into a field with huge, humped straw bales. 'So, you want to come to America?' Lucy said.

'I can't stand it here any more.'

She looked around at the rolling hills, the streams, the browns and greens blending into the Tuscan landscape. 'But it's beautiful here.'

Osvaldo started running, like a child escaping from an imaginary ogre; across the field, down a hill and up the side of the opposite hill. Lucy ran after him.

He turned to her, panting slightly, and then looked down the hill in the direction of the Donati villa. 'When I was little, I thought this was . . . well it was . . . a paradise. Our house was at the centre of the world. My parents had a lot of important friends, well known politicians bending down to kiss me, all that. Then, two years ago, one night at dinner, some men came to the door and asked to speak to my father and they took him away to jail.'

'God . . .' Lucy looked at Osvaldo in astonishment. 'Why?'

'Corruption,' he said flatly. 'Behind this beautiful life were bribes and corruption. And my father was part of the whole mess.'

'An ambulance came a little while ago and took Alex. That's where Diana and Ian have gone.' Lucy lit a cigarette mournfully. 'Where is he now?'

'Who?'

'Your father.'

'In Santa Domingo. Hiding in a new life.'

They were walking now along a dusty road lined with cypress trees. 'It's all so fucked up,' Lucy said. 'People say they love each other and then they go away. What? Do they just forget?'

'You forgot me,' Osvaldo said.

'No, I didn't. I just didn't recognise you. I remember you. You were smaller. You used to wear a hunting hat, everywhere, all the time.'

'Yes, I did.' Osvaldo was pleased she had remembered the hunting hat. He stopped walking and looked at Lucy. 'I wrote you once.'

'You did not,' Lucy said. 'I'd remember that.'

'I didn't sign it, so you probably thought it was from Niccolo.'

'What was it about?'

Osvaldo shrugged. 'I don't know. How much I liked you. How I thought of you when I was in the woods.'

'That letter?' Lucy stared at Osvaldo wide-eyed. '*You* wrote that? I can't believe it. I loved that letter. I know the whole thing by heart.'

Osvaldo laughed and started running away again. 'Dear Lucy . . .' he called back into the breeze, 'I'm sitting on top of a hill alone with my dog and I'm thinking of you . . .'

'Hey, wait.' Lucy ran after him.

Osvaldo fell, laughing and gasping for breath, under a giant tree. 'This is my tree.'

Lucy sat down next to him. 'God, it's like an umbrella.'

She lit another cigarette and they sat, looking at the sun just beginning to disappear behind the opposite hill, not saying anything.

'You taught me how to smoke,' Osvaldo said eventually.

'But you don't smoke.'

'You showed me how to inhale and then gave

171

the cigarette back to me. I smoked because your mouth had been on it.'

'You did?' Lucy was saddened. 'I don't remember.' She thought how much Niccolo's letter had meant to her, how she'd treasured it, and how she had crept into Niccolo's room and breathed in the scent of him. And, all the time, it had been Osvaldo's letter, Osvaldo's room, Osvaldo's shirts . . .

Suddenly she began to cry. Osvaldo, not used to girls' tears, put an arm cautiously around her shoulders. Lucy wiped her face angrily. 'I never cry like this. But when the ambulance came, it was so awful. People die and then what, you're supposed to stop caring?'

'I know,' Osvaldo said.

'People just accept it. I don't see how . . .' She pulled away from him abruptly. 'Sorry. I feel like an idiot.'

'Everyone feels like an idiot,' Osvaldo said. 'At least if they're not one.' He wished she hadn't moved away from him like that, and wondered whether he should put his arm around her again. 'Our parents,' he said bitterly, 'they've given us this world and they don't even remember what it was like to be young.' He looked at Lucy's tear-stained face. 'You must miss your mother.'

'The worst thing . . . the awful thing . . . sometimes I can't even picture her face.' She stood up and began crying again, quietly and deeply. Osvaldo rose and, without thinking, took her in his arms. She pressed her face into his chest and it

172

seemed to her the safest place in the world. Osvaldo tightened his embrace and Lucy, looking up at him, saw that there were tears in his eyes.

She was almost laughing as she said: 'Why are you crying?'

Osvaldo looked embarrassed. 'For us,' he said.

Miranda dumped Richard at the station. She didn't even get out of the car. Goodbye was a dangerous, final word; she refused to say it in case she weakened. But she felt lighter in both head and heart as she drove back to the farmhouse. Her mother was in the kitchen, as usual, busying around with a cheese slicer, and Monsieur Guillaume was sitting at the table, looking hopefully towards her. Miranda often wondered if Diana really got off on this earth mother thing. All that cooking and caring and giving was a real change from New York where Me mattered most. How do *I* feel today? Am *I* successful? Am *I* happy? Am *I* fulfilled? Perhaps, Miranda thought, it was more fulfilling to be The Person Everyone Relies On (unpaid) than an executive cog in some multi-million dollar company? It seemed unlikely. She leaned against the counter and watched her mother slice. 'Was it awful . . . at the hospital?'

Diana didn't look up. Her eyes were puffy and she didn't think she could cope with sympathy. 'Well, we had to hang about and fill in lots of forms and they've asked us to bring in some food for Alex.'

'Don't they feed you in Italian hospitals?' Miranda said.

'Basic, I gather. Evidently they like the patient's dear ones to help out with the nursing and the feeding.'

'So, of course, your mother is already making broths and puréeing fruits,' Monsieur Guillaume said.

'I can drive over,' Miranda said, 'sometime . . .'

'I hated leaving him there.' Diana looked around the kitchen. 'Doesn't it feel strange? Empty, somehow? Daisy's in bed. Christopher's at the computer. Noemi's having dinner with Michele, if they bother to eat. Ian hasn't left the studio since we got back from hospital. Lucy's disappeared and I'm making Guy a scrimpy little meal.' She suddenly realised there was another member of the party unaccounted for. 'Where's Richard?'

'I put him on the train to Pisa,' Miranda said.

'Just now? He's gone?'

'I asked him to. I've had it with him.'

Monsieur Guillaume nodded approvingly and Diana said: 'Good for you, darling.'

Miranda looked at her mother gratefully. 'I can already picture him next summer on some island in Maine with a WASP heiress.'

'He wasn't right for you,' Diana said. Or any other woman with a modicum of intelligence, she might have added, but thought better of it. 'Too immature.'

'I'm just thinking,' Miranda said, 'that maybe I might start up my own business when I get back to New York.'

Diana looked up, interested. 'Doing?'

174

'Jewellery design,' Miranda said. 'There's this guy who's offered to back me and . . .'

She was interrupted by Christopher, coming into the kitchen carrying Alex's tray piled with broken china and debris. He dumped it on the table. 'I found this outside the cottage. Where is everybody?' He opened the fridge, looking to see what was on offer.

'Gone,' Miranda said.

'How about some chips?' Christopher said, bringing out a frozen packet. 'And have we got any chops or hamburgers?'

'Bread and cheese,' Diana said firmly, cutting two more portions of dolcelatte and ciabatta. She went over to the table, took the tray and tipped the broken cutlery and medicine bottles into the waste bin. She felt a sharp stab of sorrow; as though she was throwing away the last relics of Alex's presence. Glancing out of the window, she saw Lucy coming along the terrace carrying a huge bunch of wild flowers, her hair blowing in the breeze, her cheeks glowing with fresh air and what looked to Diana extraordinarily like real happiness.

And then she noticed that a young man . . . Gregory? . . . no, Osvaldo Donati . . . had also come onto the terrace. She saw Lucy kiss him on the cheek and say something and then Osvaldo nodded and reluctantly turned to leave. She watched him go off and then come bounding back to kiss Lucy quickly on the mouth. For the first time that day, Diana smiled.

CHAPTER TWELVE

Lucy picked up the clock on the bedside table. It was 1 a.m. She'd been thinking about Alex, about Osvaldo, and about her father – her real father. Conflicting emotions that made it impossible to sleep. She got out of bed and went over to the window. Light shone from Ian's studio. She pulled on her jeans and a sweater, took the wild flowers out of the jug on her bureau, and tucked Marta's photo into her pocket.

He looked up as she came in, grey-faced and haggard from working late. 'Lucy?'

She took out the photograph and held it out. 'It's Mummy, isn't it?'

Ian forced himself to look at the picture. 'It could be . . .'

Lucy took the picture from him and put it back into her pocket. 'Were you ever in a war?'

'The strife we called it . . . in Ireland.' He wasn't sure where these questions were leading and concentrated his attention on the sculpture.

'You know, I thought Carlo Lisca was my father,' Lucy said.

'Your father?' Ian gently stroked the contours of a wooden cheek; he didn't look at Lucy.

'There's something my mother wrote about

being in an olive grove with a man with an accent and he's killed a viper and he feeds her an olive leaf and he's been in a war and he has a wife,' Lucy said, all in a rush. 'Do you remember where you were in August 1975?'

Ian turned to face her. 'We'd just bought the house in the spring of that year. So . . . we'd have been here, I think. Is that when that picture was taken?'

'No,' Lucy said, 'I mean, I don't know. It was when I was conceived.'

'When you were conceived?'

Lucy hardly heard, she was wandering around the room, picking up an object here and there. 'What?'

'Nothing.' Ian gazed thoughtfully at the ground.

'You looked as though . . .'

'No, I was just thinking.'

'What?'

'That must be when I did your mother's portrait.'

Her feet brushed against a pile of old junk in the corner of the studio. Lucy looked down. There, among the bits and pieces, covered in sawdust, was a pair of worn, high-heeled green sandals. 'That's what I thought,' she said.

'I could ask Diana,' Ian said suddenly. 'She'd remember. But come to think of it, she was in London then, working out her divorce and the custody of the kids, so she'd probably be no help. It was one of the only times we've been apart . . .'

'No,' Lucy said quickly. 'I wouldn't ask Diana.' She looked up, straight into Ian's eyes and then, lightening the tension between them, put the wild flowers down on the table. 'I brought these for you.' She came closer. 'So, am I done?'

'What? Oh, almost.'

'Can I see now?'

He put out a hand to hold her back. 'If I show it to you, it will be our secret.'

'Okay.' Lucy looked at Ian's hand and then at her own; the same long, delicate, tapering fingers. She understood.

'You can keep a secret, can't you?' he said.

'I think so.' He looked so anxious that she smiled at him reassuringly. 'I learned from a master.'

Ian put an arm tightly around Lucy and held her close to him for a moment, and then, arm in arm, they stepped together towards the sculpture. 'How did you get to be such a lovely girl?' he said.

Diana was sitting slumped at the kitchen table, too tired to go to bed. Every time she closed her eyes she saw, as though the scene was imprinted on her eyelids, Alex tidily pinned down by white sheets and obscene rubber tubes. Even though he'd attempted a jaunty thumbs-up sign, he had seemed a stranger. Elegant, witty Alex, whose friendship she had cherished for so many years, had left her already. In his place was a diminished figure, a hospital patient. She hadn't even recognised him. 'He's over there,' the nurse had told her, 'the bed by the window.'

She looked up wearily as Ian came in. 'So, she turned out all right?'

'Who?' Ian paused in the doorway.

'Your Lucy,' Diana said. She'd known for years, of course, but hadn't wanted to acknowledge it. When Sarah had brought Lucy to stay four years ago ... the three of them together. And then, the other day, seeing Lucy and Daisy, the two heads bent over the book.

Ian closed his eyes. This was what he had feared most. 'She's fine ...' he began. He and Diana so rarely talked about the things that really mattered and he would give anything not to have to do so now. He opened his eyes and looked at the woman he loved sitting there, forlorn. 'She's ...'

Diana interrupted before he could say anything more. She knew that she and Ian hovered on the brink of an emotional quicksand. Who knew if, once in, they'd ever come out of it? 'I'm getting tired of taking care of people,' she said.

Ian felt as though he was drowning in relief. She knows and she's not going to say anything, he thought. Thank God. 'But you're so good with people.' He came over, sat down next to Diana and took her hand.

She looked at him bleakly but gripped his hand as if she was afraid of losing him. 'Am I? Do you remember the time we were in Carrara?'

'When?'

'Right after we met.'

A memory stirred at the back of Ian's mind ... 'The quarry?'

'We were walking past this narrow bit. And you held onto my arm and kind of drew us along.'

'Did I? How heroic of me. I wish I remembered.'

'You're lucky not to remember things,' Diana said. 'I wish I didn't.' There was a pause while Ian sought a safe reply. Before he could think of anything appropriate, Diana said: 'I want to leave here, Ian.'

'What?' Ian looked at her, astonished.

'Here.'

'Leave here?'

'Yes,' Diana said. 'I want to go home.'

'This is home.'

'Not really.'

'But, this is where Daisy was born.' It seemed to Ian an irrefutable reason for staying.

'It's not the same, Ian, any more. Everything's changed, somehow. I don't want to die here. I want to die where I belong.'

Ian thought he understood. 'You're upset about Alex. It's awful, love, I know, but moving's not going to change that . . .'

Diana didn't seem to be listening. 'I want to go back to where it's grey and damp and the milk doesn't go off, where there are no television towers on the next hill. I want to go. I feel . . . I'm not . . . *this* any more. It's over. It's as if was all a dream . . .'

'A very long dream,' Ian said. 'It's no good, Diana, we can't go back. We tried to sell once before, remember? It can't be done.'

Diana withdrew her hand. 'All right, all right. We'll talk about it later.' Ian stood up. 'Are you going back to work?'

There was something, a softness and pleading in her voice, that gave him hope. 'Well, I was going to . . . but if you want me?'

'No, no,' Diana said. 'I was going to ask you turn on the irrigation. It was parched today.'

'Right. I will.' Ian went to the door: ' 'Night, then.'

Diana went over to the dresser and picked up a photograph of herself and Sarah. She put out a hand and covered Sarah's face, and then she covered her own.

Lucy was smiling as she pedalled towards the Donati villa in the moonlight. She felt a wholeness, a sense of peace she'd never experienced before. She parked the bike in the courtyard, tiptoed over to Osvaldo's window and tentatively threw a stone. And then another, and another. Finally, she picked up a big one and tossed it firmly.

Osvaldo, who had been asleep, woke up and went over to the window. 'Lucy?'

'Were you asleep?'

He reached down and pulled her up into the room. 'No, no.'

'It was so quiet,' she said, 'without Alex in the next room.'

'I'm glad you came,' he said. 'How did you know this was my room?'

Lucy didn't answer. 'It's a nice room. I just found out something kind of big and I wanted . . . I wanted to see you.'

'What was it?' They were standing facing each other, uncertainly.

'Well, it's kind of a secret,' Lucy said, 'but maybe I can . . . sometime . . . if I get to know you better. Then I'll tell you. I thought it would be this big thing, but it's different than I thought.'

She looked around the room, and then at her hands. Osvaldo, perplexed, took one of them and rubbed it. 'I'm shy with you.'

'Me, too,' Lucy said. 'But also, not.'

'No?'

'I mean, I guess I am, too.'

Osvaldo tucked her hair behind her ear and was about to kiss her, but lost his nerve. 'Is there a moon?'

Lucy looked out of the window. 'It's gone behind the clouds.'

As she turned back, Osvaldo did kiss her. They were in an awkward position, their noses seemed to get in the way, but neither of them dared move. Lucy didn't mind the noses. This was nothing like the practised kisses Niccolo had given her; Osvaldo's kisses were tender and she could feel a responsive warm glow surging through her body.

'Do the stings hurt?' Osvaldo touched Lucy's chest diffidently. She pressed his hand there and they kissed again, this time urgently, with rising passion.

Suddenly Osvaldo drew away. 'So,' he looked at Lucy reproachfully, 'who was that guy last night?'

'He needed a place to stay,' Lucy said, 'and it

182

made everyone happy. He stayed in my room, but I slept on the couch.'

Osvaldo led her towards his bed. 'Don't sleep on the couch tonight.'

Lucy pushed off her shoes and they lay back on the bed, kissing. It seemed to her the most natural thing in the world when Osvaldo took off her sweater, kissed her breasts and slipped his hand under her jeans. She shrugged out of them and he caressed her. 'You like this? Is okay?'

'Oh yes . . . yes . . .' Lucy was amazed, swooning. 'I never did that before.' Flushing, her hand reached his fly and held him.

Osvaldo pulled off his T-shirt and shorts and pressed his chest against her. He kissed her again and then tried to enter her. It was painful but Lucy didn't care. She wanted this to happen. It felt right.

Osvaldo saw her wince and pulled away. 'Should I . . . ?'

Lucy held him closer, not wanting him to stop. 'No, it's okay.'

He got on top of her, fumbling. 'Could you . . . with your hand . . . ?'

She guided him inside her. It hurt at first and then it didn't and she was overwhelmed by waves of pleasure. They were both breathing heavily, almost panting. He came with a little cry and fell against her. Lucy wrapped her arms around him and held him close. What was it she'd told Alex that first night, when he'd told her she was in need of a ravisher? I'm waiting, she'd said. She wished she could tell him now that she had finally found what she had been waiting for.

Osvaldo looked up and saw that she was smiling radiantly. He hugged her tightly to him, and when he started to shift, she laughed breathlessly and grabbed him back. 'No. Stay.' They fell asleep in each other's arms.

Lucy was standing at the window, dressed. Osvaldo, a sheet around his waist, had his arms around her. 'Do you have to go?' He put his hands under her sweater, caressing her back.

She kissed him. 'I'll see you later.'

Osvaldo suddenly looked serious. 'I want to come with you.'

'Now?'

'No. To America.'

Lucy clung to him. It was what she'd hoped he'd say. 'Then do.'

He kissed her again, tenderly, and she dropped from the window and stood there, looking up at him.

Osvaldo hung out of the window. 'It was my first time, too.'

He watched Lucy cycle away across the vineyard.

The wind whirled her hair across her face for a moment, blinding her, then it blew the hair away from her eyes and she could see.